The Witch's Revenge

The Witch's Revenge

Second Edition

Thank you for Everything!
Casey J. Oliver-Martinez

Casey J. Oliver

TATE PUBLISHING
AND ENTERPRISES, LLC

Published by Tate Publishing & Enterprises, LLC
127 E. Trade Center Terrace | Mustang, Oklahoma 73064 USA
1.888.361.9473 | www.tatepublishing.com

Tate Publishing is committed to excellence in the publishing industry. The company reflects the philosophy established by the founders, based on Psalm 68:11,
"The Lord gave the word and great was the company of those who published it."

Published in the United States of America

ISBN: 978-1-68118-017-5
1. Fiction / General
2. Fiction / Occult & Supernatural
15.01.02

I would like to take this opportunity to thank those people who made this book possible. First, to my children, who waited so patiently for this book to come to fruition. I love you, and this volume is humbly dedicated to you all.

To my mother, whom has supported me and encouraged me in every silly thing that I took into my head to do. Thank you, and I love you.

To my loving husband, Jason. You have backed me up and supported me so much, that I don't know what I ever did without you.

And last, but certainly not least, to my dear friends.

Thank you for sitting on my bed and listening to the same chapter week after week every time I changed a single word.

Prologue

The witch trials of Salem village have always fascinated me, even as a child. It is for this reason that I chose to write this book. Most names are accurate, Sara Goode was one of the first three to be arrested, tried and ultimately, executed. I was able to locate some of the names of her children and Samuel Goode was among them. I was unable to discover much more, as historians seem to have lost interest after the year 1711. To give some background on Sara Goode, the heroin of our story, she was something of a female tramp that had the nasty habit of bearing many children and then farming them out to various families in the village.

She would go door to door, begging food and tobacco for her pipe. Her husband, Samuel, did odd jobs throughout the village, yet did not have a real trade to speak of. Ann Putnam was one of the girls whom accused Sara Goode and many others. She did, in August of 1706, make a public apology before the congregation, and was accepted back into the fold.

There were many, however, that felt that the apology was a sham. A way to save the tattered remains of her reputation in the face of scorn.

Rever and Samuel Parris is very real, and it was in his household that his daughter, Betty and niece, Abigail, began their love affair with witchcraft, being inducted into the occult by the household's slave, Tituba.

The historical accounts of this manuscript are true and correct to the best of my abilities, being the product of many hours of research. The remainder is pure fiction, fluffed up for entertainment value. I do hope that I do not anger any of the historical figures mentioned in this book, lest I should be the next victim of The Witch's Revenge.

Chapter One

I realize now that I must resign myself to leaving my home. As far back as I can recall, I have lived with my family in a small mountain town in northern New Mexico. I have been happy here, as the pace of life is languid and relaxed. Exactly what a member of my particular character would appreciate in a suitable homestead. I cannot believe that my family would actually welcome the opportunity to abandon our comfortable life here. I had always assumed that they were as content as myself with our life. We currently live in a moderately sized, ranch-style home that I have always assumed has suited our needs adequately. Now, we are to relocate to a place that I assume is very far away that my family refers to as a "Massachusetts".

I enjoy my life here. My days are often consumed with a wide plethora of activities that I find most entertaining. Chasing jackrabbits through the sagebrush, bathing in the warm sunlight, climbing the many aspen trees that surround our home to languish on a branch for hours, feeling the cool mountain breeze that moves over me. Yes, I shall miss it all. I shall especially miss the mice. The abundant rodent population that bursts forth from the landscape in every size imaginable. Small, medium, large, as though I were ordering from a take-out menu designed just for me.

Perhaps I should introduce myself, lest you should think I am some demented child with a penchant for rodents. I am a feline. Not cat, that word has always offended me. It conveys our species, yet not totally encompasses the beauty, charm or intellect of our race. I do believe that the word feline is far more appropriate.

I regard myself as a superb specimen of a gray long hair of indeterminate origins. My name? Is Bubbles. An absurd moniker thrust upon me by my sweet, simple-minded family the moment that they rescued me from that most disagreeable place called the "pet store". That heroic rescue is what accounts for my fierce loyalty to my family. My one regret is that I have been unable to show them what life is really all about. Unfortunately, they are always too busy to stop and receive their lesson. I have no children, having been altered at the appropriate age to prevent such situations from arising. As such, I prefer not to be referred to as a specific gender, as I believe this practice is nonsense when one is unable to procreate. I often wonder, however, what it would be life to have a brood of my own. This momentary lapse of reason is often brought about when I have spied one of the parents of the family looking with pride upon one of the children and I see the love and contentment in their faces. I sit and daydream about what might have been, thinking at the same moment that it was rude to be rendered thus without my permission or opinion. But, alas, it is quite often at this precise moment that one of the children does something that makes me cringe, such as breaking a lamp, or spilling grape juice on the beige carpeting and I am reminded that I am indeed lucky that I have been spared the inevitable migraines.

I apologize, for I digress. At the present moment, the family is in the dining room, discussing their plans to move "east". I have no idea what this means, as I never did take a very keen interest in geography. I have far more important matters that require my immediate attention.

I am often astounded by the number of tasks I must complete for the greater food of the household. I am often needed to lie on the carpet in the family room for a great many hours a day. This is to ensure that it does not roll up and cause an injury. Other instances, I am required to dispose of the family's table scraps, so as to keep the household waste production to a minimum. Add to that the various other chores that are required of any other household pet, such as lying on the beds to ensure that the coverlet does not escape, chasing insects that only we can see to prevent an invisible infestation, and sitting on our humans' laps to as to anchor them in the proper spot for a few hours of relaxation that they may not otherwise allow themselves, and it does begin to seem that the list never ends. I am kept quite busy with the business of protecting my family and their possessions.

Why, in point of fact, I am so accomplished that

they are often not aware of the full purpose of my activities. I believe myself to be invaluable to my family, and one of my few complaints is that they do not seem to realize it.

My family, the Hanson's, are a loveable group.

The mother, Julia, is particularly kind. She is delicate boned, with thick dark hair. This is contrasted beautifully with her piercing, light blue eyes. Being feline, I am no judge of human beauty: however, I do believe that Julia is a lovely creature. She is quite intelligent, and one of her favorite activities is reading. I often join her, sitting on her lap for hours as she reads the works of Tolstoy, Fitzgerald, Shakespeare, and others.

This is what accounts for my rather extensive vocabulary beyond "meow". Roger, the father, is friendly enough. A strapping human male, dark of hair and eye, he posses a muscular build that enables him to perform the heavy lifting, so to speak. He can have a rather surly disposition, and when he has a bee in his bonnet, I have noticed that it often takes Julia a good deal of time to calm him. I am not permitted near Roger until he has had ample opportunity to change from his office attire. I find this most insulting, as I do consider feline hair to be quite the attractive accessory in any right.

The family's youngest child, Toby, I am rather fond of, having been acquired shortly after his second birthday. He takes after his father in looks, yet has the overwhelmingly good fortune to have his mother's eyes. My only complaint where Toby is concerned is that he does have the tendency to handle me a little on the rough side. A rambunctious nine-year-old, he never seems to stay still. He participates in a wide variety of sports as an outlet for his enormous quantities of energy. In point of fact, the only time that Toby stays in one place is when he is watching his favorite sport, soccer, on television. This sport eludes me, as it seems to me that it is nothing more than silly humans, running up and down a large yard, chasing a ball that is not attached to a string or even filled with cat nip.

The eldest child, Christine, is ninety-eight years old, or fourteen in human years. An accomplished dancer in the form of ballet. In this regard, she is fortunate to take after her mother's delicate boned frame. She is a bright, beautiful child who possesses not only good looks, but vase amounts of intelligence for one so young. I thoroughly enjoy lying upon her bed and watching her practice. I do believe that at these times, she most resembles a feline, and her grace and poise never cease to astound me.

I have deduced the state of my plight from conversation that I have overheard whilst prowling beneath the table during family meal-times, searching for any bit of food that has valiantly escaped the family's plates, and therefore must be devoured for the infidel that it is. I resent the fact that this is the manner in which I must gain my information. Though am quite accomplished in espionage, I wish the family would understand that I would much rather be consulted directly. As a being of higher than normal intelligence, I might have been able to offer advice, perhaps a solution or two, anything other than this drastic measure that the family foolishly presumes to be practical. I have come to the realization that humans do not understand that we felines do have a brain in our heads, and therefore, would appreciate being regarded as the extraordinary beings that we are. I do believe that humans presume that we think of nothing but chasing mice and playing with those absurd things that do a poor job of masquerading as kitty toys. I have come to the rather frightening conclusion that my family means to follow through with this insanity. I will admit here that I always presumed that they were as happy as myself here, however, from what I understand, Roger has managed to secure a far more lucrative position that will allow Julia to stay home in pursuit of her dream career as a writer. As she is also with child again, I can see how Roger believes this to be vital.

What I cannot comprehend is why they feel we must go so far away to accomplish this. For the remainder of the week, all is chaos. Carefully organized by Julia, of course. Roger refuses to lose control of anything and he is under the rather erroneous assumption that he is the one who runs our tight little ship. Everything is being run on a tight, non-negotiable schedule, so as to prepare us for our rather expeditious departure. Various chores are attended to at alarming speed, and it seems to me as though everything is whizzing by in one great blur.

Cartons have been obtained and are filled to bursting with belongings. These are then carefully labeled and stacked. Piles of old newspapers are used to wrap delicate objects, and the scent of old paper and ink hangs like a fog over the entire house. Every day, another room has been picked apart, packed and organized, the items either hidden within the confines of a box or shrouded in white sheets. I hardly recognize my home anymore. I have lived here for the better part of seven years and there is nothing here to connect the chaotic present to my happy and content past.

By the end of the week, there is nothing to connect this empty shell with the happy home that it once was. Everything save for the bare essentials for living has been wrapped, packed and labeled. I had hopped that, in the chaos, I would not have to visit my physician. Unfortunately, my false sense of security was shattered the day before our departure. My physician, a sniveling little snip of a man aptly named Mr. Tweed, is one of the few humans I detest. With his bad teeth and thick glasses, he exudes the rather disagreeable aroma of garlic and onions. It does seem to me as though he derives a kind of pleasure at prying open my jaws and examining my mouth and teeth until it is dry and I am left to attempt to gather a suitable degree of moisture. He pokes and prods for what seems like hours, examining portions of my anatomy even I had forgotten that I possess, if I had even been aware that I possessed them in the first place.

The torture and torment continued for an indeterminate amount of time, forever would be an accurate description. At long last, I was pronounced fit for travel. I know that I should have been pleased with this insignificant parasite's little stamp of approval; however, I was preoccupied with plotting how to scratch out his eyes, a suitable punishment for the indignity I had just suffered.

The present dilemma was how to get past his glasses, as those monstrosities must weigh in at a good twenty pounds. My owners were negotiating the purchase of a large carrying vessel, a portable prison of sorts, made of beige plastic and bars. I am appalled that I am to confined to this contraption as though I have committed some gruesome crime. A common criminal I am not.

The most embarrassing mistake I have ever made was as a kitten. I made the rather embarrassing faux pas of presenting my mistress with what I considered to be a prime specimen of a prairie dog. In my naïve state of mind, I assumed that this was a suitable gift, A token of my appreciation for the heroic rescue of yours furry truly from the pet store. I would have preferred to have the ability to purchase costly gifts, however, one is limited when one possesses a serious lack of finances and opposable thumbs. Therefore, I felt a rodent to be a perfect substitute for the diamond earrings that I would much rather have given. That particular foray cost me a visit to Mr. Tweed, whom proceeded to stick me with little needles that he shoved under my skin. A torture technique that I believe he called "Shots". Had I been able to speak, I would have confessed to taking the Lindbergh baby.

The day of our departure dawned sunny and pleasant, and I was rather disappointed that this lovely day was to be consumed with work instead of the pleasure that such a day demands. A large white van arrived while I was in the kitchen having my morning meal. I was attempting to delay the inevitable by taking my time and thoroughly devouring every last morsel. I was very aware of the two male voices accompanied in the dining room by Julia. She was instructing them as to which items were to be placed into their vehicle. She sounded a mite frazzled , and I determined that she must be in need of my assistance. I decided to move into the living room upon finishing my meal, assuming that this would be the optimal position from which to supervise. I observed the men, large and beefy to the point of deformity, and I sauntered to my position. I should not be critical, as I am the stereotypical, pudgy house pet. Roger was instructing the men to move his antique collection to the rented moving trailer that was attached to the rear of the family vehicle. He loves that collection more than life itself, to the point of carrying it across the country on his own back rather than entrusting it to these two cretins.

I watched intently, to ensure that no mistakes were being made. This was a delicate task, and I was pleasantly surprised to note that things were running smoothly. The children were lending a hand, Roger was helping the men, and Julia was finishing packing the remainder of the family belongings. We, Julia and I, had taken on the difficult task of aiding in the division of the possessions. A rather strenuous activity, I assure you.

I began to marvel at the mens tireless energy. I could not believe that they could do all this, without so much as a cream break. I assume that I was astounded as I tire at anything more strenuous than chasing a fly. I do not understand, nor am I entirely sure I would want to, the human concepts of "work" and "jobs". I simply cannot comprehend the exertion of that much effort when important, truly important, matters require one's attention. Naps, lounging, pouncing, why the feline mind boggles with the many dire errands we must complete for the sake of humanity.

I do believe that the only times in a human life when they truly understand what is important in this world is infancy and their golden years. It is during these two periods that they understand the importance of naps, meals, lounging, and the pondering of invisible insects. The meaning of the word "hurry" is lost on them, and I admire their ability to comprehend the many aspects that tend to plague the life of a feline. No, it is between these two periods that they lost sight of what truly matters. They are so busy rushing off somewhere that they have no idea what they are missing.

Their lives are taken, nay, consumed, with appointments, work, school, soccer practice, ballet, meetings, shopping, errands, bills, taxes, brownie meetings, cub scouts, school plays, PTA, lunch dates, dinner dates, goodness! Their lives are spent just trying to survive the next fifteen minutes.

Even meals are rushed now. Pre-packaged, time saving products rule their diets. No one savors the flavor. If they cannot microwave it, or prepare it in twenty minutes, they would rather go hungry. This distresses me. I do believe that dining is not only one of the many pleasures in life, but an art form to be studied, practiced and perfected.

As I am pondering this, milling over the complexity of this all-important issue, Julia approaches me with a dish. I was delighted to discover that it contained a rather large helping of my favorite meal. This struck me as odd at the time. I had already dined that morning, however, seeing as my philosophy is "waste not, want not", I decided not to squabble. I can say that this life practice is what accounts for my rather generous physique. Coupled with the fact that I believe in maintaining the image of the plump family pet, so as to add an element of continuity to the lives of my humans. With this thought, I dove in, so to speak. The flavor was a bit strange, but not wholly unpleasant. Perhaps Julia had added something extra in appreciation for my valuable services.

Upon finishing, I thought it best that I resumed my managerial duties. No doubt the family had come to chaos in my absence. I was relieved to see that nothing was in shambles, and I noted most everything that was in need of my careful supervision was completed. I wished I could have given them each a gold star. I began to feel utterly exhausted, no doubt from the tireless effort that I was exterting. I wondered if they really could finish the remainder without me. Upon assessing the progress, I supposed that they could do fine on their own and determined a light nap would restore my strength. No doubt my services would be sorely needed later.

Chapter Two

I awoke in a rather cold place on a hard surface. I felt groggy and my head hurt. Struggling to comprehend the reason for this, I felt like the kitty version of Rip van Winkle. I say up on my haunches, despite the dizziness that resulted from this sudden movement. A series of criss-crossed bars slowly came into focus in front of me and beyond that, a window. It was at this moment I realized that I was in the carrying vessel. I must have ingested a sedative! No doubt at the suggestion of Mr. Tweed. That odorous scrap of a human being. I was annoyed by this, as I would have entered the vessel freely, had someone had the foresight to ask me. I do realize, however, that my family is human enough not to have recognized that we felines are sensible creatures who respond beautifully to reason and logic. I therefore forgave their momentary lapse of reason.

I peered between the bars of my temporary prison to see out of the window. The mountains to which I had become so accustomed had disappeared and in their stead was a vast land of nothingness. I was just beginning to wonder just where in all felinedom we were when I overheard Roger say something about a "Wichita". I pondered as to what that could be, however, the typical avenues of discovery were quite obviously closed to me. As such, I decided that there was little more to do than wait and see. Sighing, I wondered what I could do to amuse myself. Unfortunately, my family did not think to put a worthy tome in with me, thus, I was unable to engage in the one activity that may have saved my sanity. Having failed that, I wondered what I could do to amuse myself. What does one do in prison? I suppose I could have attempted to exercise, as I have seen fictional prisoners do on television, but this required a most disagreeable exertion of effort on my part. Realizing that I felt rather grimy as an after effect of the drug, I decided to content myself with a bath to clear my head. Turning to clean along my spine more effectively, I noticed to my surprise and delight that a good deal of edibles had been placed on the interior of my cell. I suppose that this was to appease me once I had discovered my state of confinement. I chuckled to myself in delight at the gesture, as none was needed. I understand that humans do not comprehend that we felines hold no grudges. We simply know that humans are limited in the capacity of reason and logic and therefore, must be tolerated with vast amounts of patience.

The children were in the rear seat, closest to me, each occupying themselves with their music players and inane adolescent reading material that masquerades as in-depth journalism. Roger was driving, fiddling with the radio, and I could hear him complaining to Julia about the length of the drive.

"If I had known it was going to take so long, we would have given them everything and flown!" His gruff voice rang throughout the car. "Roge, you knew it was going to take this long.

The movers said it was a three or four day drive." Julia was reading one of her gardening magazines as she spoke, and her tone implied that she was bored with Roger's complaints.

"Oh sure. But three or four days doesn't seem like a long time until you are actually driving it. I mean, there are no landmarks here. It just doesn't seem like we are going anywhere."

He located a suitable station that was playing that awful noise that humans like to call "classic rock". Stifling a sigh, Julia said, "I know, it does seem to stretch on forever, doesn't it? Well, we will be in Wichita soon. What do you say we stop there for the night? Lord knows, I am hungry and I am sure the kids would like to take a swim after the heat." Aha! I thought, so, this Wichita thing is a city. That proves to be the light at the end of my tunnel. I would certainly be pleased to be liberated from my cell.

"Julia, are you sure you want to do that? I mean, there is so much that we need to do, especially in a house that big. I mean, it's practically a mansion.

Besides, I have to be in the office on Monday, ready to go, and we can't really afford to waste any time." Roger said.

"Nonsense, Roger, and you know it. We have the rest of the week. You know full well that I can do everything once we get there and the furniture is moved in. Besides, the kids are tired, I'm tired and you won't be ready to go Monday if you're exhausted. Plus, I am sure Bubbles will need to be let out soon."

At last, someone had remembered that I exist.

And I had thought they had forgotten about me.

Roger sighed, "Alright. We'll stop. I guess you're right, but I am not stopping tomorrow until I am about ready to pass out. I want to be sure that we are there when the movers arrive. God only knows how they will do things if we are not there. They'll probably break something." He had assented with his usual grace and decorum. He may bring home the bacon, but Roger is certainly aware of who puts it on his plate.

It was at precisely this moment that I noticed that I had finally gotten over the after effects of the drug. I thought it would be wise to remind my family of my presence with a soft "meow". Christine put down her version of reading and swiveled around in her seat to pet and placate me until we arrived at our destination. The sky had begun to grow dark, the sunset unmarred by the presence of mountains. Suddenly, the lights of a city came into view, and I was beyond relief that I would soon be freed.

I came to understand that Wichita is a metropolis. An incredibly large populace plunked down in the very center of the flattest land I had ever set my eyes upon. The sight truly astounded me and my little jaw hit the floor of my cage in utter, speechless surprise. As we drove, I noted the rather large river running through the center of this city. Julia took this opportunity to give the children a cultural lesson by telling them that the city was built on the fork of two rivers, in accordance with a Native American belief that this would protect them from "Tornadoes", whatever that is.

We spent some time, looking for a suitable place to bed down for the evening. At long last, we came upon a rather large building that Roger called a "hotel". I had no idea what that meant until we were settled in. Apparently, these building are nothing more than a series of bedrooms, built for the sole purpose of housing traveling humans. Roger began to sift through a large book, attempting to locate a suitable establishment to supply the family's supper. The family squabbled over what to eat, finally deciding on pizza, and placed their order. The children went downstairs to make use of the pool while they waited for dinner to arrive. I had no idea what a pool was, until I looked out of the window. Apparently, a "pool" is a large bathtub of sorts that humans swim about in. The whole notion seems rather disagreeable to me. We felines are not known for being overly fond of water, and to be totally immersed in it seemed a rather odd way to pass the time.

I made use of my portable facilities and decided that I would allow myself the pleasure of laying upon Julia's lap for affection. I was not disappointed. She immediately began to scratch between my ears, and I allowed myself to doze. The meal arrived soon, and Roger went down to fetch the children. I noted a rather disagreeable odor clinging to their skin and hair, and deduced that this "pool" must be filled with stagnant water. And this is what humans do for recreation! I would rather chase a ball of yarn. I lay on the floor; I am not permitted near the family whilst they are dining, and patiently waited for any tasty scrap that may make it's way down to me. The family was discussing the remainder of our journey, planning in advance for the next day's length of the drive. Roger said he would like to pass through a "Tennessee" so as to see a "Graceland". The children groaned and rolled their eyes. From this reaction, I realized that his desire stemmed from his obsession with a man named Elvis. I did not particularly care what the family did, as I had already come to the conclusion that I was to be confined to that thing regardless.

When they had finished their meal, they decided that it would be relaxing to use a "hot tub". From the talk, I concluded that this was a smaller "pool" filled with heated, stagnant water. I marvel at humans. Using such methods to relax. They obviously have yet to discover the therapeutic qualities of a good belly scratch.

After they departed, I was left to my own devices. I thought it wise to retire to the open carrying vessel, so as to avoid having to ingest another sedative. To pass the time before blissfully drifting off to sleep, I let my mind wander. What awaited us at the end of our journey? What would our new home be like? My real concern was what the rodent population was like? The sport of our former home was always a welcome distraction, and I did hope to continue a modified version in our new residence.

I fell asleep pondering many such important questions.

Morning came far too soon to suit my taste.

Bright and early, Roger began to hustle the family to "get a move on". I yawned and looked about me, please to note that someone had already closed the door to my cell. I was not looking forward to another day in solitary confinement, however, one must make do in such situations.

The family was bustling about the room. Showers were taken, teeth brushed, and possessions packed. The flurry of activity impressed me, and I myself was not in such a hurry to say goodbye to sleep. If this black cloud indeed have a silver lining, it was thus: that my confined state allowed me to be sedentary and continue with my sleep despite the activity around me. In the midst of all this, Julia remembered I might want to be fed, and gave me my breakfast. I must say the service was well worth a tip, but alas,

I had left my wallet my other pants. Or, I would have if I had pants. At last, we were herded out to the vehicle and continued on our way.

The family breakfast was of the fast-food variety, and I was allowed to dispose of the uneaten scraps.

It pleased me that I was allowed to continue my duties, even in this limited capacity. We had already left the city limits by the time the sun was fully up. I was not agreeable to have been awoken so early in the day. I did hope that this did not become a habit.

Roger was still insisting that we go through Tennessee, however, the children responded in the same fashion as the night before, and the subject was quickly dropped.

The land passing by my window was even more uneventful than the day before, and I was growing increasingly tired with the monotony of it all.

Roger persisted in his plan to continue until he was ready to stop, and Julia agreed. She had managed to dissuade him yesterday, and she when to hold and when to fold.

"This way, we only have one more day until we reach Salem." Roger was still trying to convince her of his brilliance I suppose, although, it did not seem to be entirely working.

I do not know what a "Salem" is, but I do hope it is something pleasant. I tire of the so, as one is limited in the capacity of entertainment when one is thus confined. The children were bickering again, and this I was quickly tiring of as well.

Roger's complaints and valiant plans to keep us moving were scraping upon every raw nerve I possessed. Most of all, I was tiring of Julia's efforts to keep the peace.

Seeing as I was not to be liberated anytime soon, I decided to entertain myself. I suppose I could have pondered the meaning of life, however, I had pondered this very quandary to the point of nervosa, always coming to the same conclusion. That being, we felines are the only creatures with enough foresight to understand this concept. I could have plotted my escape, but any plan I could deduce required the use of opposable thumbs. As a result, that was out of the question. I had long ago grown tired of the childrens attempts to amuse me, and they were now engrossed in their own activities at any rate. As all other options had failed me, I decided that the best method of distraction was sleep. I had been aroused rather early, and everyone knows that felines do not function well on too little sleep. A nap was certainly well in order. Perhaps when I awoke, I could think of something better.

When I finally did awake, I noted immediately that the sky was dark and filled with stars. I had no idea of how long I had slept, but that question was rather moot when one had such beautiful heavenly bodies to marvel at.

I heard low voices, a note of urgency folded within them. Seeing as the children were asleep near me, I perked my ears further to hear the parents. The tone was most urgent, and I knew this was something of the utmost importance.

"Julia, I know this is a great thing. I know the kids will be pleased too, but let's get serious for just a minute and really think about this. I mean, that many new additions to the house are going to get really rough, financially speaking. Are you sure this is as good as it seems?"

What could he be talking about? New additions? I thought Julia was only having one baby.

"Look, I know that this seems sudden..." But he did not allow her to finish. "Seems sudden? Julia, we are more than half-way there. It is sudden, very sudden. Here we are in the middle of nowhere and we get a call telling us that we have to take in two more cats and four horses. For the love of reason, they knew this was was part of the deal before we bought the place. They decide to call us with this little 'development' when we are already on our way. I mean, come on. Had we known ahead of time, we could have thought about it, but this way, we are kinda stuck!"

He had almost forgotten himself, and was about

to raise his voice when Julia gave him a hard,

"Shhhhhh!"

"I know that it does not seem right, and I know that it seems like a lot. Roger, please, will you just listen for a change? Mrs. Mahoney said that they are used to grazing, so that means the horses are taken care of. There are plenty of grounds, so that also means they will not be in the way. As for the cars, come on. Two more is not that big of a deal. The price has not gone up on account of this, and I really don't see why you are being so stubborn." She was upset now. Roger has a tendency of blowing things out of proportion, and Julia could only stand so much.

"That sounds all well and good, Julia, but can we get back to reality for a split second? Those horses have to cost a lot for shoeing and health care.

That's issue number one. And Bubbles is a glutton as it is. If those two cats are anything like that, we will be broke inside of a year!"

Well, I never! I am not a glutton! I just believe in the relaxing properties of a good meal, is all. A philosophy you should consider giving a try, big boy!

"Roger, that is nothing but a load of nonsense and you know it. The health expenses for the horses may be on the pricey side, but they won't need it more than once a year. And while I agree that Bubbles may be something of a glutton, you make it sound as though you have caught him red-handed in the cookie jar. Besides, this may be a great opportunity for him to shed a few pounds." And she was supposed to be on MY side! "Two more won't be much of a problem. I promise, it won't be as terrible as you make it sound."

"Well, maybe. All I am saying is that it is going to take quite a bit of readjustment. By the way, did Mrs. Mahoney say what the horse were?"

Roger was giving way, and I just knew that the worst was yet to come. Julia paused and sighed.

Then she threw out the words like they were little ticking time bombs. "A Shetland pony and three Clydsdales." She waited, as did I, for the inevitable explosion. To our mutual surprise, it never came. Roger merely shook his head and sighed. "Well, I suppose that we can go along with this insanity, at least until they start to be a problem. If that happens, I am sorry, hon, but they will have to go."

Julia pounced, "Roger, I think everything will be okay, but I agree. If they start to become a burden, we will find different homes for them." She was obviously pleased with herself. Roger had agreed, and with no bloodshed nor teeth pulled. But I knew the real reason that he had assented so gracefully. Christine had been hinting for some time that she had wanted to learn to ride horseback. Her relationship with her father had been strained as of late. I believe that Roger had assumed that this would cure the pained feelings that he assumed he was causing with his daughter. I do not think that he was aware that at Christine's age, all children become slightly estranged from their parents. I do not know the reason for this, nor would I ever pretend to. However, I do believe that in time, she will come around and appreciate her parents for what they are.

I am not pleased with the prospect of having to share my life with additional felines. I could not comprehend that the family was apparently not only going to accept these intruders, but it seemed as though they were actually welcoming the stranger. Embracing them, if you will. I could not understand their enthusiasm. Having been the only pet of the family for several years now, I have become a singular creature, adopting this trait into my very nature. I suppose that I should have been thinking of how to make the best of a bad situation. In hindsight, however, all I could do was nurse my wounded pride. I was appalled that I was to be replaced. My indignation knew no bounds, and I could not help but feel the stab of pain to my heart at the very thought that I was not appreciated as I should be. I could not believe they were going to sweep me under the rug. I was a good and loyal pet, completing my duties with little complaint. Why, I did not even sharpen my claws on the furniture. I kept the household together. Often was I called upon to console the children when the parents could not reach out to them. Many was the time I have been there to aid Julia through the mood swings that accompany her condition and come without warning.

I had no idea when we left our home that this situation would come into play. Why, if I had, I would not have stayed, so as to make room for the new pets. Perhaps they had realized this, and chose not to inform me on this matter, as they had done countless times before.

I mulled over these thoughts for what seemed like hours. I began to see lights in the distance, evidence of a city. What do I care for another night in a hotel room? I was about to be replaced by my family. The very idea of new pets caused a great gray cloud of depression to descend upon me like a heavy fog. I imagine that this is what the sky must feel like before the onset of a great storm. First, I lose the home that I adores, and then my family. If I was to be abandoned, to be thrown to the four winds, than I decided to play along for the time being. My ears perked suddenly, for I lighted upon the idea that would save me from this lunacy. I could stop this injustice. I could prevent my own demise. I would maintain my current bond with my family, and strengthen it, if possible. When they see me for the model pet that I am, so to speak, they will not be so quick to replace me with new ones. They would not want to push me aside. I vowed at that moment to be the perfect traveling companion. I would not complain, I would not fuss. If I can make them believe that I was the perfect pet, perhaps I would not have to worry about these new creatures that were trying to weasel their way into my family's hearts. By Jove, it was so crazy, it just might work! I would persist. I would triumph!, I fell to sleep with a rather smug, self-satisfied grin on my cute, furry little kitty face.

Chapter Three

The remainder of our journey I spent doing everything felinely possible to impress the family.

I did not meow nor caterwaul. I did not stir from my cell in our hotel rooms, except to handle the obvious calls of nature. I preoccupied myself during the long drives with the dilemma that awaited me at our final destination. I was not inclined to accept the fact that two more felines would be pushing their way into my comfortable little world. My status as beloved pet was firmly fixed for some time now, and I enjoyed it. As a result, I pledged my loyalty to the family in grateful return for their kindness and generosity. I would do all within my power to keep them from harm. Not an easy task, let me assure you. I have found that humans can be rather self-destructive if left to their own devices. If I am to share my home with these two felines, rest assured, it was not to be an equal partnership. I made the decision that upon our arrival to our new home, I would set the boundaries that were to be followed by my two "companions" and myself.

The issue of occupying myself was solved with devising my plan of attack. This was a tad on the difficult side, however, for I had no notion of what lay ahead. It is a dilemma when one is trying to plan a counter attack when one hasn't the slightest notion how the initial assault will be carried out. This must be what Winston Churchill felt like. I swirled this problem about in my head, considering every option I thought possible. I carried on whole conversations in my head where I established my seniority and they seceded, recognizing my undisputed claim. At least I was able to keep boredom at bay.

I soon discovered that a "Salem" was our destination. I was astounded by the green beauty of it, and when Roger and Julia rolled down the windows, I detected a hint of salt in the air. "We must be really close to the ocean." Julia said, sighing in pleasure from the scent lingering in the air. "Yep, this is certainly not a place you would have expected to be connected to witches." Roger said.

"Witches?" Christine asked. Julia was proud of her daughter's curiosity, seeing it as a sign of an inquisitive mind. "Well, sweetie. In the early 1690's, Salem became famous for trying and executing people that they thought were witches. Twenty-two people died because of a group of girls. Actually, I think most of them were right around your own age, and thought it would be fun to accuse people who had upset them of witchcraft."

One trait I admire in Julia is her belief that children should not be lied to, and often told them thing the way they were instead of sugar coating it. Christine sat back and digested this for a moment, obviously troubled by the fact that so many people had died as a result of a game played by girls her own age. "Mom," she said, "Why would they do something like that? I mean, didn't their parents do anything?"

Her discomfort with this thought showed, and I could not blame her for that. Who would not be upon learning that someone as young as twelve or fourteen held so many lives in their hands. Considering the mentality of most children of that age, I must admit, a shiver or two went down my spine.

"Chris, honey, those were different times, and people did not always use common sense. If you want, we can research it. Maybe that will help you understand it a little more."

Roger stopped the car in front of a large brick building and disappeared inside. While we waited, we all took a look at our surroundings, taking in the cobblestone, the large trees, and the warm sunlight playing off of such. When he returned, he carried with him a large yellow envelope, and was grinning like the Cheshire cat. Settling back into the driver's seat, he handed the envelope to Julia whom proceeded to shuffle through the contents.

"Well, you were right/" He said. "The price didn't go up on account of the horses, so I guess we can keep them." He was obviously pleased that he did not have to dig any deeper into his pockets.

Christine began to wiggle in her seat and there was a gleam in her eyes. Once she had gotten a hold of herself, she squeaked, "Horses? Do we have horses, Daddy?" Even from behind, I could tell that Roger was grinning from ear to ear. His hero status had been restored, for the time being, at least.

"That's right, princess. I didn't want to tell you

last night, because we didn't know what was going to happen today. I know that you have wanted to learn to ride, and I didn't want to get your hopes up until we knew for sure." Julia was giving him a hard look, upset that he was taking credit for her idea. He got the message, and cleared his throat before continuing. "When we are finished settling in, we will start looking for someone to teach you to ride. Sound like a plan?" Christine was gasping for air, her excitement belied by the sudden intake of breath, and the lack of breathable oxygen for the rest of us in the car. Toby merely snorted and rolled his eyes. A typical gesture where anything involving his sister was concerned.

We continued on our way through the town, and I was thoroughly impressed with the quaint architecture, the size of the populace not nearly as large as that of the town we had left behind. The people looked friendly enough, and they watched us go by with curiosity and pleasure upon their faces. Newcomers, the look in their eyes seemed to say. I half expected them to stop us in the middle of the street and roll out the welcome wagon. The streets were clean and in good repair, the flower boxes clearly tended often. The charm and warmth of this place struck me, and for a brief moment, I was not homesick.

After a time, we began to drive down a rather lengthy road, lined on either side with tall stately trees. The majesty of the place was quite overwhelming, and I could not but be a little pleased with the way things had turned up thus far.

I may have been completely unaware of what awaited us at the end of the road, however, for the time being, I had to admit that perhaps this had not been quite the, shall e say, bad idea that I had originally envisioned. I listened intently to the conversation that was going on amongst the family, hoping that the information I sought concerning the local rodent population would be included. Unfortunately, my humans were woefully unconcerned on this all- important matter, and went right on discussing their trivial concerns of wallpaper, yard space, and where the local grocery was located.

"We're not that far from town. Only about ten minutes or so. That will come in handy when school starts this year." Roger was weighing and calculating information. Analyzing and already planning his morning routine so as to get the maximum amount of tasks done before heading out to the office. This is a habit that I have always detested, simply because I do not see why he needs to weigh and measure every second of his day.

Moments later, the tree lined road ended abruptly at a large circular drive. A stately home squatted beneath a ring of trees as though it were waiting for something. The large expanse of lawn was green and sparkled with the dew of the morning and ended a few feet from the house. In the center of this emerald beauty was a long dirt trail that led up to a wraparound porch built of whitewashed lattice. Roger slowed the car to a halt. Contrary to my expectations, no one moved a muscle.

"My goodness." Julia breathed. "It's even more

beautiful than the internet pictures." Her eyes were glued to this massive structure of red bricks and white pillars. "Yes, I'd say it was well worth taking in two more cats and a few horses." Roger said, even as I cringed at the disagreeable term. He continue, ignorant to the fact that I had been offended. "It says here their names are Nigel and Periwinkle." He was removing the contents of the envelope, obviously looking for something. He grumbled and muttered, removing piles of paper that one would not think could fit into such a container.

"So," I thought to myself. "This is Massachusetts? Doesn't look too bad." I will admit, what I could see from my cage was quite beautiful. I supposed I could tolerate living here, provided that I could find as many lovely distractions as I am accustomed to.

The moment was shattered by Toby. "Nigel?"

He inquired, a note of disgust tainting his voice.

"Who names a cat Nigel?" Toby was in the blatantly sarcastic stage of his growth. "Well, sweetie," Julia's voice had taken on that tired, matronly tone that she only used when her nerves were frayed, "I believe that the previous owners were from England. Nigel is a common name there, for cats and for humans."

Her willful son was about to pursue the matter further, until Julia gave him one of her hard stares that silenced him. Instead, he settled for crossing his arms and huffing to make his disdain known. We exited the vehicle with an unusual amount of pandemonium. I was emancipated from my prison and allowed to walk about freely for the first time in what seemed like years. Stretching luxuriously on the lawn, my muscles began to release the stiffness from the cramped quarters.

I suppose the family expected me to roam and frolic, however, curiosity got the best of me, despite the old cliché. I rushed up the front steps. They had been whitewashed as well, and from the scent that clung to them, I guessed that the chore had been completed recently. The porch was a good three feet off of the ground with a swing bench attached securely to the ceiling of the structure. The beautiful view invited one to sit and do nothing for a while. The front door was a massive creation of dark, red-brown wood. A rather plain design graced the front of this monstrosity, and the door knocker was a graceful, heavy thing of iron. Roger produced the key and we were permitted the first interior look of our new home.

I stood for a moment in the doorway, caught breathless by the sight of the foyer. Dark, hard wood floors polished to a gleam greeted us. The staircase rested in the middle of this room, grand and sloping, with a breezeway on either side. The banisters were painted a blinding white, a pleasant contrast to the dark wood that permeated the house. The children burst through the door with the fervent energy that I have always felt was wasted on the young. I padded softly in, eager to explore this enormous place. The first look from the outside had not prepared me for a home of this size, and I was astounded by the amount of space that was here. I surveyed my new home, hoping to get a sense of where I should explore first. To either side of me were large, expansive rooms that obviously led somewhere. To my left was a large doorway, and I entered. A beautifully appointed parlor with a rich, dark green fabric covering the walls greeted me. At the front of the room were two massive windows. I could envision a pair of antique benches with soft cushions in front where I could nap. The wall to the right of this one was also consumed by windows, affording an excellent view of the grounds. The rear wall was almost completely taken by a massive stone fireplace. This would prove most welcome on a chilly December morning. The final wall of this room contained floor to ceiling shelves, and I could envision them housing a proper library.

I was most pleased with our new home thus far, and fervently hoped that the remainder was as equally impressive. To the right of the foyer was the family dining room. Again, the wall that made up the front of the house was all but consumed with two imposing windows. Here the walls were covered with a deep blue fabric. Directly opposite from the doorway was a second stone fireplace, on either side of which were two doors with no knobs with which to open them. I wondered how one might gain access to the rooms beyond.

Trotting across the room, I put up a paw to scratch lightly at the door, a gesture I often used to signal to the family I wished entrance. I was most surprised when the door gave way on it's own, and proceeded to push my rather substantial weight into the next room.

Here was a sunny, well-appointed kitchen that had quite obviously been recently renovated. Many more windows permitted the sun through, and the overall effect was sunny and cheerful when combined with the bright, canary yellow pain. White tile graced the floors and the center of the kitchen was filled with a rather large island that served as an additional workspace. I proceeded through the kitchen towards the rear of the house, and there was permitted entry to another room. This was smaller, with a bench that wrapped around one corner at the other end of it, directly below another set of windows. As I moved my gaze up, I noted that two whole walls and part of the ceiling directly above the bench were nothing but windows. I quickly deduced that this was something of a breakfast room, and noted the family's dinette set would do here nicely.

At the joiner of these two rooms was a small, slim door. Obviously an entrance to a pantry of sorts. I marveled at the amount of light that streamed into these two room. A beautiful and arresting sight, I can assure you. I was most pleased with the appointments of our new home. I made a mental note to assure that Julia would see to the benches having proper cushions. I knew that I would enjoy napping there upon finishing my morning meal.

It was during the course of this thought process that I suddenly felt something at my back. My whiskers began to twitch in a most disagreeable sort of way, and the fur along my spine began to bristle. My ears perked, and yet I could not detect any sound within my immediate range. However, the reactions I was experiencing put the message through loud and clear. I was not alone in this room!

Chapter Four

To end your quite obvious suspense, I will describe what transpired. Upon my realization that I was not alone, I quite cautiously turned about in order to discover the source of the sensations I was on the receiving end of. I am not known for my enjoyment of being attached, and as such, wish to avoid it at all costs. I am not a big fan of surprises, either, and felt that it would be most embarrassing should I have a near fatal heart attack on our first day in our new home.

I perked my ears as high as they would allow.

Being attached to my body, that was not very much higher than they already were. I had hopes that I could detect what the presence was. Noting a hint of movement just around the corner of the kitchen island, I determined that it would be far better to be the surpriser than the surprisee. I began to move as quietly as possible, so as to attack first, should this thing be dangerous. I was just about to round the corner when I noted the distinct scent of a feline.

Lo and behold, such a creature came upon me with such suddenness that we almost bumped heads! This feline was quite a bit older than myself, not so wide of girth, with black fur that ended abruptly in a patch of white on his chest.

Gray patches dotted his coat, and I determined that this must be one of the felines I would henceforth be forced to live with. His droopy gray whiskers twitched, and a deep voice reverberated throughout the kitchen. "Good Afternoon." The British accent struck me immediately, and I determined this must be Nigel.

"I suppose that introductions are in order." I was most eager to begin my task of keeping my place in the family. As such, I responded, "No introductions are needed for you, sir. I do believe that you are Nigel." His fur bristled slightly, and I could tell that I had already offended him. A slight annoyance of our species, we are forced to wear our hearts on our sleeves, so to speak. "My name is Nigel, yes. My full entitlement is Nigel Jameson III. I am the butler of this house. I will be most glad to assist you in any way that you may have need." His tone implied that I was little more than a dullard, and I must say that I was taken aback. His nose began to sniff the air, and his ears perked. The look upon his face asking the question that he dared not voice aloud. I felt that the best course of action would be to answer his unspoken quarry.

"I assure you, my motives for residing here are completely benign. I have absolutely no intention of treat you as a servant, nor do I intend to do so with any other creature that resides here. You are a servant no longer, and must become accustomed to behaving as just another ordinary household pet."

I had hoped that this statement would clear the air, however, the look with which he regarded me was as if I had just committed some dreadful crime. His lip curled with obvious distaste, and momentarily, I assumed he would simply walk away from my. My hopes were dashed, for he stayed on and looked upon me as one would a mouse.

"I have very strict mannerisms, sir. I do believe that there is nothing that one could call an 'ordinary household pet'. I believe that all should earn their keep, and I have no intention of simply lazing about. I have been in this mode of service for a great many years, and have no intention of becoming the stereotypical household cat that sits about all day and expects his comfort delivered to him as though he were household gentry. No sir, I may no longer be a butler in title, but I shall always be one in manner."

The nerve of this glorified tomcat! Why, I was being told, in no uncertain terms, mind you, his assessment of me. We had not even been acquainted a full five minutes!

"Now, see here, sir. I am not going to simply stand here and be insulted. Nor will I allow you to make unfounded assessments of my position. I do not simply lie about, expecting my comforts be brought to me. I perform a great many services for my family, sir, and I will not permit your most obvious disdain."

I am quite sure that my indignation was belied by my tone, yet I could not help myself. I was upset with this feline's erroneous charge of my and my purposes, and was quite determined to set the record straight before it got out of hand.

Nigel looked shocked indeed, and took a deep breath before speaking. "Do try to understand, sir. I meant no offense. As I have stated before, I have been in this position for so long, that is has practically become second nature. I did not mean to impugn your position on your family. I do believe that we have started off on the wrong paw, so to speak. In the interest of making amends, might I five you atour of your new home?"

I understood that he was attempting to clear the tension that had descended upon us, and it would have been impolite, nay, boorish, to not make an equal effort. I felt that a tour with a feline that had resided here for many years would be quite a bit more informative than one on my own. Alas, there was still one item that needed to be cleared before we could begin.

"Yes, I do believe that would be most helpful.

However, do not bother calling me 'sir' or 'madam'. I do not label myself a specific gender, for I have been disabled in the capacity of procreation. I tolerate such nonsense from my family. I am sure you are as painfully aware as myself that humans are quite fond of labeling everything they come into contact with. I prefer to be addressed by my name."

He nodded solemnly, indicating that he understood my plight. I appreciated that we seemed to have gotten back on track so quickly. "May I inquire as to what I may call you?" His tone was one of curiosity, a lovely change from the obvious snobbery of only moments before. "Bubbles." I replied, somewhat embarrassed. "A ridiculous name, I am aware. However, it is the product of a seven year old girl, and I do believe that we mustn't argue with children."

Nigel nodded in understanding and said, "It is tiresome. It does seem humans are so unoriginal when it comes to the names of their pets. I wonder that they never ask us what title might be agreeable to our mind." It was the first, and few, instances in which I would ever hear Nigel criticize humans. He continued, "Now, shall I show you about the house?" He was doing his best to be cordial, and I thought it would only be civil to reciprocate. "Certainly. It will be lovely to not have to draw my own conclusions."

We exited the kitchen, going back through the dining room and into the foyer. "Have you seen the parlor?" He asked, and we paused, deciding where we still needed to inspect. "Yes," I replied, "But I have yet to see the upstairs portion of the house." "Very well, we shall begin there." He said as he began to lead the way up the stairs. "Now, this portion of the house is the original structure. The kitchen and breakfast nook were added on in 1924. The dining room was the original keeping room, or kitchen. The family would use the fireplace to do all their cooking, and this is the reason that the fireplace still contains the original hook." I was admiring the thick, maroon carpeting on the stairs, and he continued his history lesson. "My master purchased this home from the last remaining descendant of the original owner. I believe they had the surname of Goode. As such, the original portions of this structure date back to the year 1696. It was built four years after that ridiculous hysteria that caused the deaths of twenty-two supposed witches. I still, to this very day, marvel that all the madness began with but a single egg."

I had no idea what he meant by this, and was about to inquire as to the importance of eggs, (anything that has to do with food captivates my attention), but he continued, leaving little room for interruptions. "Apparently, the man who built this house was the son of Sara Goode, one of the first to be tried and executed for witchcraft."

I began to wonder why I was being told all of this. We had reached the landing during the course of this history lesson, a subject I have never been particularly fond of. I have far more intriguing matters to consume my time. At present, I was most anxious to inquire as to the local rodent population. The problem seemed to be that he noted my curiosity and mistook it as my being interested in the house. We proceeded to the front of the landing, and looked down upon the first floor of the house.

We came upon a room with the door open and the first thing I noticed was the size of the chamber. A rather large room, with white walls and a soft lilac trim on the moldings. The color scheme was by far feminine in nature and Nigel spoke to this effect. "This is one of several bedrooms, no doubt the very one the young mistress will choose for her own." The chamber had ample space, and I could envision Christine's things arranged in it. The sound of the children in the backyard reached my ears and I could not but be pleased that the children seemed happy thus far with their new home.

Nigel once again broke into my mental wanderings, "Shall we continue?". This came off as more of a statement than a question. I did not appreciate the sudden return of his "Holier than Thou" attitude. However, I thought it best to hold my tongue until the opportune moment presented itself.

We moved to the room that is directly to the right of the first, and Nigel continued, unabated. "Seeing as the color scheme here is much more masculine,

I am sure that the young master will prefer these quarters. The door there is to the washroom that connects the two chambers." As much as it pained me to admit, he was correct. The room was a mix of deep reds and greens, and I could see Toby would most certainly want this for his very own. I was not, however, ready to relinquish so quickly.

"Yes, I am sure Toby will be most pleased with these accommodations." I said. "However, it does occur to me that humans are such fickle creatures, and I am quite sure they will choose their own appointments when they have an opportunity to do so." I was attempting to remind Mr. Nigel Jameson III just whom had been with the family longer and therefore, held rank above him.

"Just what are you implying?" He inquired, taking immediate offense which had, in fact, been my very goal.

"Why, nothing at all." I feigned innocence when really, I was grinning inside. "I was simply stating that the Hanson's are human, and will undoubtedly choose their own accommodations when they wish."

I was attempting to diffuse Nigel's temper for the simple reason that I did not wish to have a fur fest here in the hall. I have never been one to use brute force, and I would be hanged if this snob forced me into a confrontation that I had absolutely no desire to enter into.

To the right of "Toby's Room" There was a long corridor that stretched to the very back of the house. Nigel showed me the various rooms and chambers that resided here. Few were more than glorified closets, and there was even a room that contained a second staircase that I was informed led to the attic. I had no desire to see this room, having heard far too many tales of New England homes with bats in the rafters.

In this corridor was an entrance to the master bedroom, with a second entrance on the landing. The chamber was large, and yet, not at all imposing. A third door led to an anti-chamber that Nigel informed me was a "fainting room". I quickly calculated the proportions of said chamber, and deduced that it was perfect for a nursery. I made a mental note to bring Julia here at the end of my tour, in hopes she would draw the same conclusions as myself.

We proceeded to the end of the corridor, where it ended abruptly with a massive stained glass window. I was caught breathless by the beauty of it, noting that the colors seemed to melt together in a melody of various blues, greens and browns. No lines of lead threaded through the window and I wondered how this effect was accomplished. In a bottom corner, there was a small amount of crystal clear glass. If one stared hard enough, one could almost make out the figure of a feline. I was blatantly staring at this marvel, and I suppose this gave Nigel his cue to continue with the history lesson.

"Beautiful, don't you agree?" He inquired. I numbly nodded my head. "This particular window has been in the house since it was built. The original owner, Mr. Samuel Goode, had it commissioned in Boston. It was during this same trip that he also acquired his wife, Edith. The pattern is a bit difficult to discern at first. However, once you have seen it, you will never be able to get the image out of your mind."

Nigel's tone implied that he knew something that I did not, and I knew that he was merely waiting for me to ask. I did not, as I never was one to enjoy such obvious attempts to bait me.

"It is said that it is something of a tribute to Samuel Goode's mother, Sara. It is also said, whispered of course, that Sara Goode was the only true witch to have been executed. Alas, I do believe that is said of every poor soul that is persecuted in such a manner."

This felt as though he were deliberately attempting to frighten me. I must admit, I was more than a bit annoyed by this. Brushing him off, I found that I could not stop myself from staring at the window. The image of the feline was directly below what appeared to be human feet, suspended in mid-air. The problem was, when I attempted to follow them up to discern the rest of the pattern, the lines would blur together and vanish.

"Shall we proceed, Bubbles?" Nigel asked, an air of extreme importance cloaking him. I wondered at the moment, and many to come, if perhaps he did not suffer from an inferiority complex.

To the right of the hall was the other entrance to the master quarters. From here, we proceeded along the landing to the front of the house, directly opposite from the room that

Nigel had designated for Christine. Here there was something that appeared to be a dressing room. I took a moment to marvel at the human concept of bathrooms, as it appeared this house had an endless supply of them. It seems to me as though humans need a room specifically constructed for every activity that consumes their day. I was beginning to become annoyed with the sheer size of the place, having come from a home that could have fit into the lower level with room to spare.

"Tiresome, I know." Said Nigel, "It does seem at times that humans are simple to the point of dault, only to double back and become alarmingly complex. I do wish they would decide, as it would aid in my duties a great deal."

We began to descend the staircase, so as to give me the tour of the remaining areas of the lower level of the house. I had no doubt I would greatly need this information later. I could hear Roger and Julia instructing the movers on where they wanted things. The children were raising Cain in the backyard, obviously happy to be free of the prison that had transported us. We reached the bottom and began to circle beneath the stairs. Suddenly, I felt my fur bristle a second time. My whiskers twitched and my ears perked to a height that I momentarily feared they might fly off the top of my head. I could feel someone else near, and that someone was most definitely not human!

Chapter Five

We had almost finished touring the lower level, and still the sensation clung to me, like the scent of not-so-fresh litter. Behind the staircase itself were more doors, and I was informed of their functions. I must admit here I was hardly paying attention. Just beyond the dining room was another thin doo, and I was told it was the second entry to the pantry. Directly beneath the stairs was what appeared to be a large cupboard that turned out to be a washroom. Circling around to the left, we went beneath the landing. Here was a mud room, closet and dry storage room. In the center was yet another door that led to the back porch. We continued in this fashion, still turning in a great circle. All the while, the fur along my spine bristled on end.

The feeling was persistent, to say the least. Yet, it was not a wholly disagreeable sensation. Just annoying enough to cause my fur to stand on end as well as my nerves. My whiskers twitched, hoping to detect the source. As we walked, I could not keep my mind on Nigel's narration, although. I was unaware if this was caused by the presence, or if it was caused by the fact that Nigel is phenomenally boring. Perhaps a bit of both. I sensed that we were drawing closer to the source of my dilemma, and I was not sure if I wanted to turn tail and run. Nigel was saying something to the effect that the study was located at the end of the house, and as we proceeded in that direction, I could hear someone speaking. Naturally, I assumed that it was Julia, as the voice was decidedly feminine in pitch. I could not hear the words, yet as we drew closer, I realized it was not Julia after all. Julia does not have a pronounced cockney accent. The voice was quite nasal, and I was attempting to sort out this enigma when I discovered it was coming from the study. "Well, what did ye expect? What with the new masters 'ere and all. The very last thing we need 'round 'ere. A bunch of humans traipsin' about and steppin' on one of ye!"

What was all this? We rounded the corner into the study. A lavishly beautiful room, plenty of the dark polished wood that was as much a part of this place as the red brick. Muted tones of green covered every surface that was not wooden. One complete wall was consumed with windows, in the center of which was a pair of French doors. Needless to say, these led onto the porch as well, and the view was breathtaking. I noted that to the right, in a corner was a large, plump feline, fur tinged with blue.

"I told ye they was comin' today. You knew. Do don't be actin' so surprised that I's talkin' ya down and such. Now be gone with ya, get back to yer room, 'fore the masters be seein' ya and getting' all flustered like." Who was she talking to?

I was quite intrigued, and was wondering just what all the fuss was about. I detected a familiar note, a scent that was not unknown to me. Could it possibly be true? Had my wish been granted? The very shock of this familiar scent caused a bout of speechless idiocy that was most unbecoming. Before I had the opportunity to inquire as to the source of the pleasant scent, a high, squeaky voice interrupted my thoughts.

"But Perry. We're hungry. I was only goin' to sneak over to the pantry, real quiet like. A bit of apple, some bread perhaps, no harm done."

The plump feline turned, her rather voluminous rump making a faint swishing sound on the hard wood floor. "Mrs. Perry Winkle, may I present Bubbles, the new masters' pet." Nigel made his introductions, and I gave the customary nod that shows respect for the elders. "So, Mrs. Periwinkle, I am most pleased to make your acquaintance. I do hope that we can become associates." The fur along her spine raised and I could tell I had offended her. A perfect score! So far, I had managed to offend both her and Nigel with the first word from my mouth. What else could go wrong?

"My name is Mrs. Perry Winkle." She said, a tinge of annoyance to her voice. "You, 'owever, may call me Mrs. Winkle. I got no patience for simpletons, Bubbles. I got lots a thing t'er do and I must be getting' Roscoe 'ere off to do 'is job for a change."

She scowled at me, and I felt myself shrinking inside, like a kitten that had nursed for a second too long. "I am terribly sorry, Mrs. Winkle," I said, hoping to smooth things over. "I meant no offense. I was simply misinformed"

I peered around her. No easy feat, let me assure you. I was attempting to discover whom she had been conversing with. Imagine my surprise and delight upon my most opportune discovery of a rodent! A fine specimen of a dark gray mouse, very plump, and no doubt to be pleasing to my well seasoned palette. I lunged, pleased with the prospect of being able to hunt again. It felt like ages from the last time I was able to savor such a morsel. Suddenly, I felt a heavy thump upon my tail and landed with a most embarrassing plop upon my chin.

Mrs. Winkle strode to me, the very picture of the strict school marm, and boxed me smartly between the ears. My vision blurred momentarily.

"Now, that's not very nice, is it? Not even 'ere for more than five minutes, and tryin' to attack Roscoe already? Hmph, you folks just don't got no decency, all's to it!" Her paw was thrust in my face in the fashion of the mother to one of her insubordinate kittens.

She continued, "Roscoe 'ere is our 'andyman.

You needn't be so impolite, what with yer bein' a newcomer and all. Why I 'ave never seen such rude be'avior in all me life! A master attackin' the 'ired 'elp without so much as a 'by your leave'".

All this while, Roscoe is standing in the corner, as far from me as possible and shaking like a leaf. Mrs. Winkle, meanwhile, was not letting up on her lecture, continuing with a fervor that I have yet to see rivaled. "No sense in startin' off on the wrong paw, mind you. I mean, you might 'ave at least waited until after the introductions 'fore you start pouncin' on everyone."

My head had begun to hang in shame. If a feline could blush, I am sure I would have. I looked at poor Roscoe and felt even worse, seeing the fright in his eyes. I had certainly began on the wrong paw, so to speak, and felt that amends must be made.

"I am terribly sorry, Mr. Roscoe. I forgot myself for a moment. You see, in my former home, I had the duty of ridding the home of intruders, and I mistook you for one. I do hope that you will accept my apologies, for they are heartfelt, I assure you."

I could not believe that I was actually apologizing to a mouse, though I did feel that the gesture was warranted. Roscoe seemed to soften a bit at this, and wrung his hands. Looking at me with a mixture of fear and surprise, he seemed to be collecting himself.

"It's fine, I suppose. I can understand the mix up. I mean, I am a mouse after all. Nigel, here, did have the same reaction when he first come here. But I do ask one favor. There are a lot of animals here. Just try and remember not to attack any of us, ok?"

I felt quite horrible, having attempted to devour this obvious gentleman. "No, no. Of course not. I will remember, and again, I do apologize." I was feeling rather sheepish by this point. Having been scolded on the one paw, and then expressing sympathy to a rodent on the other.

The intriguing aspect in all of this, and my one comfort, was that the pompous Nigel Jameson III had the same gall as I. Perhaps this was the reason for his remaining silent throughout this exchange. Roscoe peered at me, his whiskers twitching and said, "That's all right. Now, off to the pantry. Got me some unfinished business that way." He began to scurry in that direction, however, Mrs. Winkle trotted over easily and placed her rather large body directly in his path, landing with an unceremonious whump.

"You'll do nothin' of the sort. I told ya I was goin' to get ya something'. Now ya just scat alon' to yer quarters, or I 'ave 'alf a mind to let Bubbles 'ere finish what was started." Roscoe yipped in surprise and scurried away to a small cranny in the wall I had not seen before. Mrs. Winkle shook her head, allowing a tired sigh to escape her. " 'ee never learns. Always wantin' to go off and do things 'ee knows 'ee shouldn't."

She shook her head again, letting on that she was just plain tired. "Now, Nigel. Why don' ya show Bubbles 'ere the rest of the grounds. I've gotta get Roscoe a bit o' somethin' 'fore 'ee goes scurryin' 'bout and givin' us all away to the new masters." She turned to leave, and then spun around to face us again. Eyeing me, Mrs. Winkle added, "Don' ya be forgettin' to tell Bubbles 'bout the gard'ner. We don't be needin' anymore scenes." And then she was gone, leaving me to Nigel to attend to.

We left the study, heading beneath the stairs and exiting through the back door that the children had left open in their haste to explore. The porch ended with three steps heading down into the yard. Beyond this, the lawn was lush and green. Sprays of planted flowers were lined along the porch. Every color one could possibly imagine was here, bursting in full bloom. The trees had clearly been tended to recently. A beautiful stream ran the full length of the property, ducking beneath a loose fence-like structure and disappearing beyond the horizon.

Mrs. Winkle's reference to the gardener was plaguing me, and I finally asked Nigel, "May I inquire as to the gardener?" He strolled in silence for a moment, digesting the question and meditating upon his answer. Finally, he replied, "His name is Digger. He maintains the grounds quite well. We have always been pleased with his work, and I do hope that in time, you will share our sentiments."

This did nothing to clear up the question as to Mrs. Winkle's insinuation. I was just about to inquire further when Nigel stopped and called out, "Mr. Digger, would you be so kind as to come up for a moment? I have someone here I would like you to meet." We were presently met with some low mutterings. "Hang on, I'll be right up." A deep gruff voice called out. I had never heard of a gardener that lived below ground before, and I was trying to make sense of all of this. Suddenly, a large brown head emerged from a mound of earth, and the voice asked, "What can I do fer ya?" Mr. Digger certainly sounded annoyed with having been interrupted.

Nigel immediately took charge. "Mr. Digger, I would like to present the new masters pet, Bubbles. Bubbles, this is Mr. Digger. He is the gardener, and a gopher." With that last statement, he gave me a hard look that I could easily interpret, and I did not like it at all. The odd creature reached below him and came up with a dirt riddled handkerchief that he wiped his paws with. "So, the new masters have finally arrived. I've been workin' hard to get everything ready. I likes to impress new people. I hope it worked. Nice to know you, Bubbles." He extended a rather grimy paw and, not wanting to appear rude, I took it. I was still stewing, as it were, at the look Nigel had given me. I understood full well the implication. He had expected me to attack! What did he take me for, some sort of country bumpkin? Shaking off the slight, I said, "I am pleased to know you, Mr. Digger." He waved his paw and said, "Never mind the mister. Nigel here is too proper for his own good. Even if he is nothing more than a glorified British snot. Name's Digger, plain and simple. That's the way we like to do things around here, plain and simple." Digger gave Nigel a look that would have frozen fire, and I gathered that these two were anything but great friends.

"At any rate, Digger, I do not wish to keep you. You were obviously doing something, and I would not want to be responsible for your falling behind."

"Well, if you won't be needin' me for awhile. But, if you do, need me that is, just call out. I'll be there." With that, he ducked back into the burrow and was gone.

I turned on Nigel, my pent up anger flaring to biblical proportions. "Really! Was that necessary? I did apologize for having attempted to attack Roscoe. I even promised him that I would not attack anyone on these grounds!" He stared at me coolly, and responded, "I honestly do not no what you mean." The very nerve!

"Oh, I think you do. Giving that look while explaining to me that Digger is a gopher. I know what a gopher is, sir. I am no kitten just taught to use the litter. At any rate, worry no longer. I have no intention of displaying a repeat performance."

My fur was standing completely along my spine, I was so angry. One wrong word from him, and we would have a fur fest here in the yard. "Forgive me. I had no opportunity to explain it to you before paw." His lame excuse only served to anger me further. "Hair balls!! You had ample opportunity on the way from the house. In point of fact, I recall asking for an explanation and being given only his name. Try another one friend, I am not buying it!" I was doing my best to appear as menacing as possible.

Nigel stared at me, "Alright! I apologize for the manner in which I made the introductions. However, I see no reason for you to become so belligerent. I did not mean to offend, I was simply attempting to make everything as clear as possible, so as to avoid another embarrassing incident for all concerned." Nigel was getting defensive, and I decided not would be the perfect time for something of a kitty council.

"Listen, Nigel, and listen close. I am only going to tell you this once. I think now would be a most opportune moment to straighten out a few items of extreme interest to us both. First and foremost, I am the family's pet. I have been so for a great many years. Therefore, I know what is in their best interest and what is not. Furthermore, I know their habits, lifestyle and temperaments. This brings me to my second point, which is that the family will choose their own appointments, and you will not influence their decisions to suit your own tastes. Third, and final, I am not ignorant. I am no kitten that you can mold to suit you. I do possess a great deal of intelligence, sir, and ask only that you attempt to recall this fact if and when you choose to speak to me again."

There, I had said my piece. All I could do now was hope that Nigel saw things in my light. However, he looked as through I had just treat mud through his catnip! He quickly composed himself, however, and said, "Fair enough. Not, allow me to spell out a few things for you. I have lived and served in this home for many years. Therefore, I know the house and grounds better than anyone. Therefore, my judgments as to the family's appointments were based on the assumption that they possessed good taste and practical minds. As such, I am merely attempting to look out for their interests and their well-being. Second, all animals here serve a function, and we do not need any of the staff being attacked. Finally, I think you should know that there have been a few odd occurrences here that I, nor anyone else for that matter, have not been able to explain." He looked rather smug at having uttered this last statement. "Such as what?" I asked, "Chains rattling? Creaky floorboards? I am well aware of ghost stories, and while I find them entertaining, I give them no credit." Nigel gave me a long look, and sighed. "No. Shadows in the parlor. Some sounds, yes, but it is not chains rattling in the night. Then of course, there is that business of the phantom feline that no humans seems able to see." He had the look of the fabled cat that ate the canary. I was annoyed by this. I never was one to appreciate egotism. "What are you talking about? Explain yourself. If I am to live in this house, I feel that I have a right to know that the family is not being led into danger." The anxiety in my voice was quit clear, and I winced when I realized that I was allowing Nigel to get under my skin.

"In good time, Bubbles. It is not something that one can explain easily. How I wish it were something simple like smoke and mirrors. It will be easier to understand once you have experienced it for yourself. Suffice to say that the occurrences are directly linked to Samuel Goode's mother. Now, what do you say to going back to the house? It is getting dark, and I would like to see that the humans have everything in order. I am sure that you are also most anxious to do so as well." He turned and strode away, giving me no choice but to follow.

Upon my return to the house, I noted that the furnishings had been placed, still shrouded in the dust covers. The beds and other personal belongings had been placed, frustratingly enough, in the very rooms that Nigel had predicted. Much still needed to be accomplished, but the family was tired, and rightfully so. "We can finish the rest tomorrow." Julia said from the parlor, where the family had gathered to rest and, I suppose, to compare notes. "For now, let's get something to eat. I don't know about anybody else, but I am starving." Naturally, the family thought this was an inspired idea, and began to gather up their various coats and things. Soon, they were out the door, and I was left to my own devices for the first time in this monstrosity.

Chapter Six

Alone. I had been left alone. I was tempted to explore this place on my own, so as to make a mental list of what needed to be done the following day. My only question was, where to start? I decided that it was best to begin in the foyer. It seemed to me that this was the center of the house. I sat there, in the middle of the dark hardwood floor, facing the door and pondering this question.

I was trying to determine what to do next. If I was to live here, I felt it necessary to know every corner. I still did not comprehend what Nigel had told me, however, I was inclined to completely dismiss it. It seemed to me as though he were simply pulling my tail.

The fur on my back stood abruptly on end, and I could feel something moving through the house. A feeling, overwhelmingly powerful, swept over me. Not a malicious feeling, but certainly an unpleasant sensation. I was suddenly desperate to find the source of this, yet I was not quite certain where to begin. It seemed to be everywhere, as though the very walls were pumping this aura into the room.

I decided that no one ever discovered anything by staying in one place. I needed to investigate. I did not know where to start. There was no direction from which I could discern an increasing amount of strength. I stood in the foyer, turning in circles, unable to think clearly. This sensation was permeating me, seeping into every fiber that I possess. I felt urgency, though I could not tell if it was my own, or that of the house.

Yes, it felt as though the very house was causing all of this, and I was unnerved by this possibility. I had to force my mind to think. In that fleeting moment, I moved towards the parlor. As I did, I was aware that this decision seemed to come from outside of myself.

Once inside the parlor, I noted something that I had not seen upon my initial inspection. The room was bi-sected by a great archway. I could feel this sensation surrounding it, and it seemed as though this were the source for all the confusion. I trotted over for a closer look.

Evidently, this wood was extremely old. It had obviously been polished many times. Not recently, as no chemical scent clung to it. Something was clinging to it, though. Cleaving desperately, and that something was what was in this house at this very moment. I judt could not put my paw on what this was all about.

"I see that you have discovered it." A voice behind me. I nearly jumped out of my fur! Turning, I said, "Oh, thank you Nigel. Because of you, I only have eight lives left!"

Nigel stood, transfixed it seemed, staring at the archway. He continued. "I can never understand what it is. I have been here a long time, and each time it happens, I try to find out what it is.

I can never figure it out though. If it wants something known, it is going about it the wrong way. What good is it to let us know that something needs to be revealed and not let us know what it is?

He was rambling. "Nigel, just what is going on around here?" I practically screeched. But he continued on as though I had not spoken. "I had hoped to have more time to explain to you. To convince you."

He was interrupted by a creaking noise. It emanated through the room. It almost sounded like a tree limb creaking under too much weight, or a rope being stretched by a hard pull, or both. The archway had begun to glow, a sickening pale blue. It was as if it were radiating some energy or force.

Nigel stood there, still, eyes staring at the thing but not seeming to see it.

"Nigel, what is happening? What are you talking about? What did you want to explain to me? NIGEL!" He did not even hear me.

Chapter Seven

I awoke the next morning, wondering immediately just what had happened the night before. My head was cloudy, like my mind was wading through a soupy fog. Not entirely unlike the feeling of being drugged. I could hear movement throughout the house. Boxes and cartons being moved to their respected rooms, possessions being unpacked and placed. Glen Miller was playing, and could be heard echoing off of the bare walls. I had chosen the upstairs corridor to retire long before the family had returned. The light feeling in my head was not passing quickly enough to suit my tastes, and I decided that a bath might aid in clearing my head. As I cleansed myself, my mind turned to the events of the previous night. Almost as quickly as it had begun, it had ceased. The sensations that had made my fur stand on end, the creaking sounds, all of it, had dropped away. The peace that descended upon the house was almost as unnerving as what had preceded it. Nigel had recovered himself. Blinking quickly, his haughty and stand-offish manner had returned full force.

My head was spinning as I attempted to make sense of all that had happened. The snobbish attitude of the two felines, the role of the other animals on the property, and then the strange occurrences in the parlor. One had to admit, that is an awful lot to contend with in the span of a single day. Just what had happened in the parlor? I milled over this problem, doing my best to find some rational explanation for the whole thing.

Perhaps, if you take into consideration that I had been confined for the better part of three days in a small cage, fatigue could explain the hallucinations. However, what of Nigel's behavior? That could not possibly have been imagined. On the other paw, he had not been very hospitable upon my arrival. His strange behavior could be a normal part of his personality. Once could go insane while attempting to explain all of this. The really trying aspect was that I had no one to speak with so as to compare my experience to theirs.

I could hear a rumbling sound, and while that seemed strange to me, I thought it could just be the motor of the moving van. No, the possessions had been delivered promptly the day before. Having eliminated that possibility, I began to think of other things that could be the source of the low, vibrating sound. Perhaps Nigel? No, after last evening, he had been avoiding me as though I had fleas. Mrs. Winkle was downstairs as well. It sounded almost like a feline purring. No, that was impossible, no one was in this part of the house but myself, and what possible reason could I have to purr at the moment? In the midst of my mental wrestling, I moved my gaze slowly upward in the direction of the stained glass window. What I saw there made my blood run cold. It actually appeared as though the feline in the window was swishing his tail. No, that just wasn't possible. It must have been a trick of the light. I blinked my eyes to clear my vision, and yet the tail was there, moving slowly back and forth. The eyes of the feline stared directly into mine. The purr had grown louder. It felt as though the sound was coming from inside my very own head! It cannot be! Have to get away.

All reason had fled my mind. The only actual thought I was able to understand was "Get out!" I ran, not caring where nor to what end. Where, if or why did not cross my mind. Just move, get away, anywhere but here. The front door was open and I bolted through it as though a rabid dog were on my tail. Down the stairs and around the corner of the house, fleeing blindly. Good Bastet! That window was moving! The barn came into view. Get to the barn! Just get to the barn, as far from that window as you can!

I ran in, doing my best to outrun the sight I had

just seen. Not looking where I was going, I ran smack into a large object. Something extremely large, and extremely solid. Dazed from the blow, I sat back hard on my rump. In front of my eyes, filling my field of vision was a large black object, white fringe draped about it. It was attached to a leg that was as thick as a tree. A long leg. My eyes followed it up, and up and oh Lord, it was attached to the biggest monster I had ever laid eyes upon! What the holy caterwaul was this thing? Not being an overly athletic creature by nature, I was appalled at the thought of having to run again. Get away. Move before it tramples you! Run, you fat bag of fur, run! "Whoa there, little fella." A deep voice resonated throughout the barn. "Nothing to be scared of. I ain't gonna hurt ya. What's all this about, anyhow?" It took a few moment for my heart to go from my throat back to it's usual place of residence in my chest. He showed me where I might get a drink of water from a long trough. When my tongue finally went back to it’s normal size, I spoke.

"Who are you?" I asked. I was wary of relating my story, for fear of appearing insane. I did not want to start off with the other animals questioning my mental state. "Name's Jimmy. I be one of the horses 'round here." This huge monster said, his voice shaking the trough that I was sitting on.

"Bubbles. I am quite happy to know you, Jimmy." I was hoping to delay the explanation that I knew I was soon going to be forced to make. "What got you so jittery, there, Bubbles? You looked like you was bein' chased down by a pack of hound dogs." Evidently, the subject was not going to drop.

"I suppose there is not going to be a game of round about with you, Jimmy. As such, I will try to explain just what startled me. However, I am not entirely sure that what happened really happened, if you follow me." I explained as best I could what I thought I had seen, and he listened. Patiently, intently, weighing every word. When I finished, he did not say anything for a few moments. I was afraid he was denying what I had said until, finally, he spoke.

"Ya know, I've seen odd things, heard odd things, myself. I didn't tell nobody, cause I knew they'd think I had gotten hold of some bad oats. I couldn't tell the barn master, he would have thought I was a few apples short of a bushel. But, I know I can tell you. There are some strange things that happen 'round here. I can tell you that."

It took me a moment to digest this information, but I felt the need to press on. "Well, what have you seen? Perhaps it can help me explain what I just encountered." I wondered to myself, what could have possibly startled this enormous beast, let alone frighten him?

"I seen a woman. A young woman. She wore a long dark dress. There was white at the end of her sleeves, white collar, white bonnet. She looked straight at me! At first, I was a little afraid. There was something, I don't know, you could just tell that she wasn't real. Not of this world, I guess you could say."

There was a loud racket outside the barn. I could hear the pounding of many more hooves. More monsters were coming!

"Listen," Jimmy said, "She had a real sad look in

her eyes. Talk to Mrs. Winkle. There ain't nothin' goes on 'round here that she don't know 'bout."

"Thank you Jimmy. It is nice to know that I have not lost my mind. I will come and see you again." I was pleased to know that I was not the only one who had seen something strange.

I left the barn, feeling rather silly at having been frightened by such a gentle beast. He really was a good fellow once you spoke with him.

I turned back to the house. My eventful morning turned over in my mind along with what Jimmy had told me. This presented a problem. I had not anticipated a haunting. At first, I had discounted Nigel's story. Yet, if a good, sensible creature such as Jimmy had seen something, I felt that I should give the dilemma some though after all. These questions consumed my mind while I made my way back to the house. I had not had my breakfast, and I never was able to concentrate when I had an empty belly.

When I got to the back porch, the door was open. No doubt the family had noticed my absence and had left it ajar so that I might enter. The sounds of unpacking had not diminished while I was gone, and I began to look for where they had left my morning meal. I would search out Mrs. Winkle when I had finished dining. Perhaps then, my head would have stopped it's spinning, and I could interview her more intelligently.

I went to the kitchen, hoping that the practice of my meals being there would carry over to our new home. To my delight, there it was. Next to the back door, as always. As I ate, I mulled over my problem. It was rather difficult, having never encountered this sort of thing before, and I had no idea how I was to go about this. I hardly tasted my meal, my mind was so preoccupied, and though I tried to concentrate on the task at hand, the problem only crept back into my thoughts and ruined any hope I had of enjoying my dining experience. This was most annoying, as I do believe anything worth doing is worth doing well.

I like to savor my meals, and this dilemma was making that impossible.

I finally gave up all hope, deciding that I would never enjoy another meal until this had all been sorted out. To avoid that shocking possibility, I went to seek out Mrs. Winkle. Beginning my search upstairs, I was of the mind that perhaps she was surveying the rooms to be sure that they were in order. I carefully checked each one, and yet I did not locate her. I was at the same time attempting to avoid Nigel. I was in no mood to withstand that test of my patience.

It is quite difficult to attempt to locate one large, voluminous feline while simultaneously doing your absolute best to avoid a pompous, obnoxious one. One does run the risk of turning a corner and literally bumping heads with the least desirable prospect.

I proceeded back down the stairs, hoping that I would locate her in the bottom level of the house. Inspecting the parlor, I still did not find Mrs. Winkle, despite my extensive search. The study revealed nothing, and though I had already been to the dining room, I decided that perhaps our paths had missed one another, and she might be there after all.

As I had predicted, there was Mrs. Winkle, dusting off the windowsills with her tail. As we had no dining table that would fit this room, it was quite empty, leaving a feeling of incompleteness that settled in the pit of one's stomach. "Well, good day, Bubbles." She said brightly. "Where 'ave you been? The masters were lookin' fer ya this mornin'. I 'eard 'bout what 'appened last night. Don't worry yerself ducky, it 'appens all the time. I'm sure it won't come to nothin'." Mrs. Winkle was bustling about the room, her rather large rear end swinging like a pendulum.

"Mrs. Winkle, I have been searching you out all morning. I have a few questions that I would like to ask you. If I am to live in this house, I do believe that I am fully entitled to an explanation. I want to know exactly what is going on around here."

I must have raised my voice, as Mrs. Winkle appeared shocked. She quickly regained her composure though, and leveling her gaze at me, said evenly, "Well, poppet. I don't know that I be the best one to tell ya. Ya know, Nigel knows more 'bout what goes on 'round 'ere than anyone. Per'aps ya should ask 'im."

Mrs. Winkle looked extremely uncomfortable, yet I persisted. I was quickly growing tired of the run around I was being given, and for a change, I was going to get some answers. She looked about the room, as though searching for a means of escape. I stepped directly in front of her. I wished her to know that she was not to be rid of me so easily.

"No, Mrs. Winkle. I have had just about enough of this. Now I want to know a few things, and I know that you have the information that I seek. I think it is just about time that you share that information with me." I glared, doing my best to let her know the proverbial jig was up.

"Well, um, alright. I guess I should be tellin' ya the truth. What with you bein' the new masters pet and all. It all started in the early part of 1692. Salem was called Salem Village in them days....."

Chapter Eight

"There was a man by the name of Reverend Parris. He had two children in his charge. His daughter, Betty, and his niece, Abigail. They were not the problem. In this household was a slave woman, Tituba. A Caribbean native that the Reverend had acquired during a stay in the islands. She was not the problem either. The problems began when Tituba began to teach the children of the household simple magic. I suppose to pass the time that often lagged in rural communities of the period. She taught them many spells, learned during her life on Barbados.

The real issue was that she did not seem to understand that children are not very good when it comes to keeping secrets, especially those as delectable as taught them by the slave woman. They began to bring friends to share in their games of sorcery, other girls that varied in age, yet none older than sixteen. They would gather in the kitchen of the Reverend's home, partaking in the spells that were cooked up there.

One day, as they were deeply engrossed in a game of divination, the trouble began that would cost the lives of so many. The game consisted of dropping egg whites into a bucket of water. Whatever shape the white took was supposed to hint as to the trade of the girl's future husband. One girl's egg white took the shape of a coffin.

Naturally, the girl became hysterical. For reasons unknown, soon all of the girls developed 'afflictions', claiming that 'specters' were poking them, pulling their hair and generally wreaking havoc.

The town was in an uproar. Witches amongst them? The whole idea seemed ludicrous. Everyone was frightened, puritans being overly suspicious people by nature. They believed quite strongly in those days. To deny the existence of witches was to deny the very existence of God. It was an unthinkable notion, to be sure. The girls began to claim that they could identify the witches simply by touching them. Witch after supposed witch was jailed. Neighbors suddenly recalled evidence of witchcraft. Evidence such as the accused walking past their fields, and the next day, the cows falling ill. On the days of trial, the accused were brought before the magistrates in the town church, which also served as a community meeting house. The unruly children were in attendance. The trials were conducted amid the screams and performances of these girls, claiming that the accused were tormenting them, taking revenge for having been exposed. Conviction upon conviction was handed down. Innocent upon innocent was strung up on Gallows Hill.

All in all, the hysteria lasted in the area of one year. When it was all over, and the good people of the town had come to their senses, twenty-two had been put to death. One had been pressed to death by the weight of many stones that were placed on his chest during a vain attempt at eliciting a confession.

One of the women to be the first condemned was Sarah Goode. An apparently contemptible person who had the rather disagreeable habit of having many children and proceeded to farm them out to any family that would take them. She would go, door to door, and beg for food and tobacco for her pipe. Ultimately, Sarah was charged and convicted.

She was executed on Gallows Hill. The builder of this house, Samuel, remembered for the rest of his life the sight of his mother's death.

When, at long last, the girl's confessed and their devices were known, the town cried out in disbelief. They had waged a war against imaginary demons. They had tried and executed many of their townsfolk, all based on the words of sorely undisciplined children.

In 1711, the state government saw fit to attempt to make amends to the families of the victims. A mere 600 pounds was divided among them. Samuel Goode used his portion to start the shipping business that ultimately built this house. He had the tree cut down from Gallows Hill, and it was used to construct the archway in the parlor, as a reminder of his mother. Shortly after his mother's death, he acquired a white long hair cat of unknown origins. The townspeople, still in the throes of idiocy, believed that cat to be Sarah Goode, come back from the dead. As a result, they killed it, so as to avoid any further torment on the part of Sarah.

Samuel grieved his mother. All his life, he mourned the loss of hers. Although she had by all rights abandoned him, he loved her. She was his mother, after all.

We do not know when the disturbances began, nor do we have any idea as to why. We do know, however, that Sarah Goode is at the root of it. Unfortunately, her intentions have yet to make themselves known to us."

Nigel finished, having come into the room when Mrs. Winkle was about to tell all. The question that presented itself was, now that I have this information, what was I to do with it?

"Okay, granted. The occurrences can only be Sarah Goode. After all, who else could it possibly be? However, now that we are all on the same page, what are we going to do about all of this? We cannot simply sit about and allow this to continue.

The children cannot possibly understand any of this. I am sure that the two of you have noticed that Julia has a slight bulge in her middle. Well, in her delicate state, she certainly cannot take anything of this nature. No, I do believe that we are going to have to handle this situation ourselves." I was hoping they would agree with me. I knew that the chances of solving this mystery alone were slim.

"What, exactly, do you propose we do? Run about trying to commune with the entity? I think not. I have far more pressing matters that require my attention. I must ensure that the family has everything under control." Nigel said, and I wondered briefly if he had forgotten the events of last night, or was purposely choosing not to acknowledge it.

"Do you mean to tell me after your little impassioned speech last night about caring only for the family and their welfare, that now you are going to just sit on your furry butt, and not lift a paw to help?"

"Listen to me, Bubbles," condescension dripped from his voice, lingering on my name. "We have existed peacefully with this thing for some time now. I am not about to go and start stirring things up when it would be best just to let it alone. No, I will not help you on this fool's errand. If you are going to waste your time looking for answers that are not there, you had best leave me out of it. I will have no part in this."

This was an outrage. We did not know what this thing was, or what it wanted. For that reason alone, it was all the more urgent. Who knew if this force were benign or malicious? Either way, it seemed logical to at least find out that much, to ensure the safety of all concerned.

I looked at Mrs. Winkle. "Well, are you going to help me, or are you just going to sit there like that glorified tomcat?" I indicated Nigel with one paw. He huffed, as though I had made some sort of bad joke. We both glared at Mrs. Winkle, both attempting to send the silent message that we were the one who was right. However, from the knowledge that I had obtained of Mrs. Winkle thus far, I knew that she would make up her own mind, when she was good and ready.

She looked at both of us, clearly turning things over in her mind. Mrs. Winkle struggled with her decision for what seemed like an eternity, her eyes darting between eyes before wandering over to the doorway. Finally, after much consideration, she said, "No."

"What?" I practically shouted. "You're not going to help? This is unbelievable. I can't understand this!"

Mrs. Winkle held up a single paw, calling for silence in that matronly fashion. "No, I am not just goin' to sit 'ere. I want to know, same as you."

Nigel was glaring at her, obviously displeased with her decision. She looked straight at him, and before he could speak to chastise her, she said, "Glare all you like, Nigel. I 'ave made up me mind.

I am not goin' to let these poor folks walk into somethin' like this. Not without doin' somethin' to 'elp. We tried when we first came 'ere to figure this out. Maybe Bubbles 'ere can do what we couldn't."

Mrs. Winkle gave a decisive nod of her head, silencing any and all reproach that Nigel may have been about to make.

In the stead of argument, he simply turned to leave. Throwing a scowl behind his back, he snorted. "Well, I have done my best to keep fools from themselves. I dust my paws of this. I will not participate in this lunacy. What do you expect? That the spirit will come to you and tell you what it wants?" I was more angry at that moment than I had ever been in my life. It was enough that he did not want to aid in the discovery, but to have him making such remarks was beyond my power to handle quietly.

"Just leave, Nigel. If you do not want to have any part in this, that's fine, but I will not listen to your insults. If you want to go about your business as though nothing is amiss, that is your decision. Do not berate us for being concerned." If he had not left at that moment, there was no telling what could have happened. As a testament to his own good sense, he waltzed out the door. Finally left to our own devices, Mrs. Winkle and I looked at each other, trying to assess what to do from here. "well, where do we begin?" I asked. "Bloody 'ell if I know, ducky." She said, as puzzled as myself. "I guess we could try to figure out exactly what is going on and why." It was as good a place as any to start. Unfortunately, we still did not know where to begin. It was not as though we could simply jaunt down to the local library and research. No, our information was going to have to be obtained through espionage. We begin to wander the house, in hopes of gaining some information from the humans.

Entering the study, Julia had joined Roger, and they were working together in the unpacking. I could hear the children upstairs, putting away their things. Roger was handing Julia books and figurines and she was dusting off the items before placing them on the shelves. I stole a glance at Mrs. Winkle, who sauntered over to Roger to peek inside the carton he was working from. She sniffed the contents and was greeted with a friendly scratch under the chin. For all of their short sightedness, humans do know how to appeal to our more basic needs.

"Well, hello there Periwinkle. Glad to see that you have decided that I am worthy of your attention." Roger said as he scratched her ears, and I could see Mrs. Winkle cringe at the mispronunciation of her name.

Julia was speaking to Roger, and I moved closer to hear what was being said. "The Historical Society wants to meet with us. They called this morning while you were seeing to the horses. Maybe they could tell us a few things about the house. Mrs. Mahoney is a member, you know." She was cheerfully putting things away. I noted that the bulge around her middle was growing larger, and was quite near to popping open the overalls she was wearing. "It would be nice to know the history of the house. Who built it, that sort of thing."

Roger rolled his eyes. He never did take an interest in Julia's obsession with history. Up to this point, I had agreed with him. Pulling a book from his box, he inspected it carefully and said, "I don't know if this is such a good idea, your hearing all of those ghost stories. I don't think that you should be upset in any way. Not right now, with the baby almost here." He was grasping at straws and he knew it.

The reasons for his protests were as clear as if they had been painted on his forehead. He was not agreeable to having people in the house, particularly old women, poking around and asking questions. Roger is not what you would call a people person, and it was for this reason that he was attempting to discourage Julia from having these ladies to the house. "Nonsense,

Roger and you know it. It would be fantastic research for my first book. You know that I don't believe in ghost stories and all that. I know why you are making such a fuss. If it will make you feel any better, I invited them for tea, so you will be at the office while they are here." She was an expert at getting her way, and Roger knew it. It would be far better for him to not fuss, lest he should displease her. At that point, I knew that Julia was likely to ask them back on his day off for an extended visit. He shrugged, agreeing to her compromise, yet I could see the smile playing on his lips. He had planned this all along! Perhaps he was not the simpleton I had always taken him for.

The obvious reason for my pleasure was the Historical Society. There were going to be people here that knew the history of the house and the area. I caught Mrs. Winkle's eye and nodded in the direction of the door, indicating for her to follow me.

We went quickly to the breakfast room. We did not wish to be disturbed, and at this time of day, this was the perfect location to avoid interruption. "This is most opportune." I said. "We will be able to sit in and listen. Perhaps we can learn a few things that may provide a clue." I was most eager to set about our task, as I hoped to have this sorted out as quickly as possible. "I agree," said Mrs. Winkle, "But, me question is, what do we do 'til then? I mean, what if it 'appens again?"

Her tone was very precise and calm, and yet I could tell that she was as nervous as myself at the prospect. It would not be very useful to have another encounter before we had more information to go on. "I suppose we shall just have to wait and see. We can stay in the foyer at night and see if it happens again. If it does, we shall investigate. I see no other option." Mrs. Winkle nodded. I must admit, however, I was not thrilled at the prospect of meeting a ghost face to face.

For the next four nights, we kept to our silent vigil in the foyer. For those nights, not a thing happened. The days were filled with activity. Unpacking, shopping for staples, rearranging furniture, the things that I would assume would be typical when humans relocate.

It was during the course of the fifth night that we hit pay dirt. The family was sound asleep, oblivious to the strange goings on of their new home. Mrs. Winkle and I were moving about the house, determined to discover the source of anything unusual that may arise. We had searched every room in the house several time over, in hopes of learning anything useful. Alas, we were unsuccessful. We were sitting in the parlor, having completed our rounds for the second time that evening. The Historical Society was not due for another few days, and we were of the mind that, should anything happen, at least we would know what to listen for.

During these nights, we never spoke. I never knew if it was from fear of alerting the presence to our vigil, thus causing it to shrink away, or triggering a violent attack. Nigel had gone to the trouble of avoiding us completely, day or night. We had not seen a strand of fur from him since the showdown in the dining room, and for this, I was extremely grateful.

At long last, it returned. For the second time, my fur bristled and my whiskers twitched. I ventured a glance at Mrs. Winkle, wondering if she felt it too.

A low throaty growl emanated from her. The creaking noise began again, softly at first, then growing in pitch until it felt as though the very air were made of it. The presence was here! More powerful than before, we felt pounded on all sides by it. Our bodies tingled from it's vibration.

I looked at Mrs. Winkle, wishing to speak, but I did not know what to say. The words caught in my throat like so much dry food. It was a lump, not allowing sound to pass, and I began to panic. My unnerved state was not helped by the look of terror in Mrs. Winkle's eyes.

She was staring at the doorway, a look of sheer horror on her face and I recall wondering briefly what could possibly elicit such a response from her. I followed her gaze, and was started to see a feline standing there. This was not Nigel. It was a feline that was no feline. Ghostly white with long hair, and I fleetingly though of Nigel's having said that Samuel Goode had once possessed such a creature.

The strange feline nodded his head, indicating that we should follow. At the start, I was far too frightened to move. I had never come into contact with anything of this nature before. Finally, I managed to loosen myself, and recalled my resolve to sort this out. I nudged Mrs. Winkle, whom at the moment seemed to be glued to the spot. She shivered, and I gathered from the look on her face that she had momentarily been in a trance.

I gestured with my head towards the door, indicating we should follow . The feline turned, effectively communicating that he was going, whether we chose to follow or not. Not wanting to lose this opportunity, I hurried after. He headed towards the stairway, and I knew that we were going to the stained glass window. I do not know how I was in possession of this knowledge, only that I knew it. He proceeded up the stairs and we followed, daring not to speak for fear of making him vanish. He continued on without so much as glancing behind him. This annoyed me rather, as it seems to me that if there was something crucial we were to know, he would be anxious to confirm our presence.

The entire atmosphere of the house had changed. The feeling was now one of sadness, instead of the comfortable feel of a home populated by a happy, healthy family. The overall aura of sorrow permeated the air, and it seemed as though it was charged with a force of some kind. A great weight of depression pressed in upon me. As we ascended higher up the stairs, it seemed to grow thicker. In fact, one could practically see it, like a fog crawling across the floor. The tension was unbearable, and I hoped that the family was not having the same experience as I. It did not seem as though they were disturbed, no sound came from any of their rooms. I was relieved to not have any of them involved. I was overwhelmed by the sadness. It was penetrating deep into my heart and I felt the sorrow that must be directly linked to the presence's trouble.

We reached the landing, and the feline proceeded down the long corridor. It wanted us to know something, of that I was absolutely certain. As we drew near, I felt weighted down by the very feel of the presence, and I was suddenly more determined than ever to see this through to the end. If for no other reason than to derive why I was being made to experience this thing.

Reaching the end of the hall, I noted that the stained glass window was lighted with the moon directly behind it. Slowing our pace instinctively, the strange feline kept walking. Before our very eyes, he went through the wall. At that exact same moment, our ghost appeared.

Chapter Nine

Her back was facing us. I was able to note that she was wearing some sort of long dark dress. A white collar and cuffs, with a snowy white bonnet. The skirt of her dress was wide and brushed against the floor, yet made no sound. Her hands were clasped in front of her, as if in silent prayer. Her back shook, and I could hear sobbing, muffled, as though she did not wish to disturb anyone and be left to her grief. My heart went out to her. Even though I did not know what troubled her, it pained me to see anyone hurt so.

I began to wonder who she was, why was she here? What could possibly trouble her? She turned, and I could see the tears streaking her pale cheeks. She was young, very young. Her pretty face was accented by strands of dark hair that had escaped the confines of her bonnet. Her eyes were the color of a storm riddled sky. I went to her. I wanted to comfort her, give her some hope in her sorrow. She bent down and stroked my back, and yet, all I could feel was a cold tingling.

Straightening, she wiped her eyes with a plain linen handkerchief. Again, her eyes turned to the window. Fresh tears spilled down her cheeks in a torrent. I could feel her pain. The hurt of centuries ran through me and I was utterly powerless to stop it. I was not entirely sure I wanted to. Information began to filter into my mind, from where I had no idea. She had done something. Something so terrible, so unbelievable, so as to condemn her here.

What could this poor, unnatural child have done that could have warranted an eternity of this much pain? Why, she was no older than Christine. Aside from the occasional sassy comment, Christine was completely incapable of doing any wrong. Images begin to flood into my mind like water bursting through a dam.

I was trying desperately to make sense of it all, to get a reign on my mind so that I could think clearly. I needed to make a complete picture from the pieces that were being pushed into my head. The rush of images into my mind was forceful, battering my senses so I could not think on my own. I was seeing through her eyes. Girls, young girls, accusations thrown about like so many stones. Violence everywhere, hysteria. Hooded figures swinging from limbs, ropes tied tightly about their necks. Unmerciful, foolish men in dark robes and powdered wigs, death handed down to all that came before them.

Suddenly, the images stopped. I looked up, searching frantically for her. She was gone, and had taken with her any hope of finding out who she was and what she wanted. The first rays of dawn were flashing through the colored glass. A symbol of hope after a most distressful evening.

The rays of light that penetrated through revealed something that I found to be most startling. I could now see the window in its entirety. There were no dividers between the different colors, no threads of metal to ensure that the window did not fall apart. The colors simply melded, swirling together, thus creating a rather disarming effect. The pattern revealed itself to me.

I suddenly understood why I was seeing it for the first time. Every other instance that I had attempted to see it, the light was not in the proper position to allow a full view. A tree, the exact one from the images. Leafless, the branches reaching into the sky like the fingers on the hand of God. A lone woman, the gender easy to distinguish from the dress, strung up with a thick rope that was lashed to the lowest limb of the tree. Hoodless, the rope wound about her neck tightly. The artistry of this window was exquisite, for the features of the face were quite easy to make out.

It was an older woman, about middle-aged I should think. Grey speckled her dark hair. Despite the aged look, and the face being contorted in a look of anguish, the features twisted in apparent agony, it was quite simple for me to comprehend. The woman in the window was not our ghost! Throughout the day, my mind was preoccupied with the events I had been privy to. Why? That particular question floated in my head more than it should have. Why was I given all of this knowledge and no clue as to what it mean? I had no clear idea what to do with what I now knew. I did know that all of this was connected to our resident spirit, and yet I had no idea how. There was still the question as to why she was still here, what was it going to take to give this young girl the peace that she surely deserved? The most puzzling aspect was, who was she? If the stained glass window was a memorial to Sarah Goode, then who was our ghost? And, what did she want?

During the course of my "ghost hunt" the family had been quite busy settling into our new home.

From what I had observed during my brief breaks from thinking, Julia had purchased a new dining set, and the children were adapting nicely to their new routines. I suspected that they would be quite comfortable with their new home once school commenced in the fall. The entire family seemed content and eager to set about their new life. Even Roger's normally surly disposition had improved, and it seemed to me that life here was agreeing with them. Unfortunately, I could not say the same for myself. I was pleased that it seemed as though they had noticed nothing out of the ordinary, and I was determined, now more than ever, to keep it that way.

The next week passed in a flurry of activity. From the conversation that I overheard during the family's meals, the children had already been enrolled in their new school and they were most eager to begin. I found this strange, as they usually complained about the prospect of academia. Roger had apparently settled into his new position nicely and Julia had begun to spend long hours in the study, typing away on her first book. I spend the time mulling over the things that the spirit had shown to me. No one in the family thought to ask me how I was adjusting to my new life here and, for a change, I was grateful for the neglect.

I realize now that I should have gone and spoken with the other animals on the property. At the time, however, the prospect never entered my mind.

Perhaps they could have shed a bit of light on my dilemma, yet I was far too consumed with the problem to think straight. The only bright spot at this point was that I had yet to see Nigel, and I was pleased with this small indulgence. I had enough to deal with without having to add his attitude problems to the mix. Mrs. Winkle and I kept ourselves busy, brainstorming at great length, attempting to glean some knowledge from our shared experience. It was all I could to do keep my sanity.

It was quite obvious that this issue was driving me to distraction. We spent many long hours, discussing the visions at great length, and still were unable to come to a conclusion. "What do ya think she 'ad in mind, tellin' ya all that?" Mrs. Winkle had not experienced anything like myself. All she had felt was a strong sense of foreboding, as though something terrible were signaled by the young girl's appearance. She had confided that the young spirit had been there for only a few moments. This confused me, as it seemed that my experience had lasted for hours.

"What do you think it all means?" she asked. "I wish I knew. I would like to know who she is. If I do not find out in the near future, I am sure that I will lose what little of my sanity I have left." I was rather agitated at the whole thing. The fact that we seemed to have far more questions than we had gained in answers was unsettling.

"So, the spirit spoke to you, did she? Well, then,

I suppose that you have the answer to all our problems." Nigel sauntered into the room. I had an immediate reaction of annoyance to his very presence. I had enough on my mind without having his condescension lingering above my head. "I thought you were not interested in anything that we may discover." I said crisply, attempting to let him know that he, and his opinions, were not welcome. "Now, if you don't mind, we have several items that we must attend to." The Historical Society would be arriving soon, and I had little time nor patience for his negative behavior.

I wanted to get to the parlor and set ourselves up in languid positions. I am most accomplished in the matter of covert operations, and I realized that the only method that would gain us any new knowledge was espionage. Therefore, it was vital that we appear as harmless and normal as possible. It was a good possibility that something said may apply to our resident specter.

"Ah, yes, the tea. Don't tell me that you actually believe that they are going to sit about and tell ghost stories. What a lark! Perhaps they shall even bring a bag of marshmallows to toast around the fireplace and swap spooky stories. I hate to burst your bubble, Bubbles, but the Historical Society is concerned with fact. They do not deal in the so- called paranormal. No, it looks as though you are going to have to stick with crystal balls and ouija boards." He strolled out, swishing his tail in the most contrary fashion. It is a testament to my unfathomable self control that I did not attack him then and there.

"Don't mind 'im, duck. 'Ees just not used to competition, is all." Mrs. Winkle was doing her best to control my outrage. I supposed that she had much the same reaction as myself to the idiotic assumptions that Nigel had just heaped upon us. I could not understand his attitude toward this. He was behaving as though this were not a pressing matter, but rather, a minor annoyance. I said as much to Mrs. Winkle.

"When we first come 'ere, 'ee was just as determined as you is now to figure it all out. 'Ee spent hours workin' on it, but the ghost ain't never appeared to 'im. I think 'ee be'aves like this on account of 'im bein' upset that you gotten further than 'im." She presented an interesting point. I was quite intrigued with the fact that Nigel was at one time as fervent as myself to solve the mystery.

It was getting late. I could see Julia placing out the tea things. She had certainly gone to a great deal of trouble, making three different kind of sandwich fillings and her berry scones. I could hear the first of the automobiles arriving. "We best get settled in the parlor." I said. "They have begun to arrive."

The Historical Society arrived in droves. A lively bunch of chattering old biddies whom apparently had nothing better to do than sit about, in one anothers' homes, and discussing historical gossip. Tea was served, and I noted that many of the ladies helped themselves quite generously to the scones.

The old women with their pill box hats and clutch handbags fussed over Julia as they gorged themselves on cucumber sandwiches and that squishy, suspicious substance that humans call gelatin. "My dear, you look beautiful. How far along are you?"

"I love what you have done with this room. Darling, you have exquisite taste."

Their chatter reminded me rather of clucking chickens. Julia had the situation well in hand, though. "Yes, yes, thank you. I asked you here simply because I adore history and I would love to know about this house." She was a no nonsense woman, and often preferred to get right to the point.

"Why, yes, dear, of course." A plump woman in a blue dress and white gloves stood. She looked like a general addressing her army. "I am sure Mrs. Mahoney here told you that the original portion of the house dates back to 1714. What is now the dining room was actually the kitchen, or keeping room, when the house was built. The builder was Samuel Goode, the eldest son of Sarah Goode, one of the women executed as a witch in 1692. After the death of his mother, Samuel fled from Salem, from reasons I am sure you understand. He went to Boston, and there begin the apprenticeship that would allow him to start the shipping business that would build this house. In 1711, the Massachusetts government decided to distribute a bit of money as restitution for the families of the victims. 600 pounds was divided up among the survivors. Samuel Goode's share came to about 7 pounds. He returned to Boston shortly after. This trip had two purposes. One was to commission the stained glass window that is now in the upstairs hall. The other was to wed his bride, Edith Corwyn. Her father was a prominent merchant in Boston, and endowed his only daughter with a dowry of a large, yet unknown, sum. The couple returned to Salem, where Samuel had built this home and proceeded to have many children. The house passed down along the generations, each adding a little here and there to the house. Finally, it reached the last descendant, Mary Goode. She lived out her life as a spinster, and from there, the Jamesons purchased the home." Julia was obviously dissatisfied with this little speech. It was apparent to me that something was weighing on her, and I wondered briefly if the old hens noticed it too. "What is troubling you, my dear? I don't suppose it was something I said." The lady in the blue dress sounded concerned.

"Oh, no. It's not what you did say, it's what you did not say that's bothering me. What I mean is, is there any history of disturbances in the house?"

She kept her tone light and even. She went so far as to take a nonchalant sip of her tea.

Julia has said it as casually as possible, and yet, the old biddies reacted as if she had shouted at them. They looked at one another, alarm spreading across their faces like so much rouge. Finally, Blue Dress cleared her throat to speak. "Well, my dear, what makes you ask?" Her voice crackled, and I gathered that this was a subject that no one wished to discuss.

"I have noticed a few odd things that have occurred throughout the house, and I would like to be sure that there is no reason to be alarmed. I am sure that there are reasonable explanations for it. You, see, my cat has been acting peculiar lately. I am not entirely sure if it is the new surroundings, or if it is something else."

Blue Dress spoke again. This time, she had regained her composure and her tone was even and controlled. "Well, dear, yes. I mean, there have been reports. We did not want to tell you. Gossip often has little bearing in truth, you know. I suppose there is no choice now. Mind you, we put no store in such things. However, the former owners of this house did say that odd things have a tendency of happening here."

The poor woman looked panicked. All of the other biddies were shifting in their seats and the sound of stiff, rustling dresses echoed through the room. "Off things?" Julia looked intrigued. "Such as what?" Much coughing and throat clearing occurred, and it was obvious that they hoped to be relieved of discussing the unpleasant subject. Julia spoke again. "My dear ladies, understand that I only ask out of curiosity. I am writing a book, and I would like to know from a purely professional standpoint. I do not frighten easily. As such, I would like to know exactly what is going on in my house." This marvelous woman could calm an angry tiger. Her words hit their mark, and Blue Dress moved to the edge of her chair before speaking.

"It shall be far easier to explain once we have told you a bit more history." I found it amusing that she said 'we', and yet, she was the only one speaking. "One of the main accusers during the trials was a girl by the name of Ann Putnam. Her mother, also named Ann, fed the child so-called information as to whom she believed to be a witch. This enabled the child to accuse them. These were people that the elder Ann felt had offended her in some way, and it was a most effective method of eliminating her enemies. She was not a very likeable person, and something of a semi-invalid. She was more often sick than not. When the other girls were trying to repent their falsehood and thus spare more deaths, the younger Ann Putnam help fast to her accusations. When Sarah Good was swinging from the gallows, Samuel Goode had told Ann she would pay for her sins. Ann mulled over this, at first dismissing it, and eventually, becoming hysterical over it. Some ten years after the trials and executions, Ann Putnam confessed before the church that she had been wrong, thus being accepted back into the congregation. It was whispered that she had confessed simply because of what Samuel Goode had said to her, and did not truly mean a word of it. She died some years later.

She never married, for who would take such a creature to wife after all that had transpired? It is said that the spirit of a young girl in a dark dress and white bonnet roams these grounds."

They knew about the ghost! What unbelievable luck! I perked my ears to hear better. "There are also reports of seeing a white cat on the grounds. A most unusual occurrence to be sure. Reportedly, Samuel had, in his youth, had such a cat before the mob killed it. They had mistaken it for Sarah Goode come back from the grave." I trotted over to Julia, intent upon sitting in her lap. I wanted to be able to hear every word said, lest they should reveal any more of our ghost. Of course, I had to endure the petting and patting of the old hens, whom thought I was 'just too adorable for words.' One must make sacrifices, especially when one is as aesthetically pleasing as I.

Julia cleared her through. "As you were saying, ladies." She was most anxious to get to the bottom of this. Mrs. Blue Dress shifted in her seat. "No one knows anything of real value with regards to these occurrences. In fact, no one really knows if they have actually happened." Julia looked a bit surprised. "What do you mean? If there have been reports, surely, there must be some truth to them."

"My dear, on some of the accounts, yes, the truth must be there. However, a majority of the reports were made by a few less than reputable people." Blue dress looked rather smug at having uttered these words. "If the persons making the reports were less than reputable, then why bother mentioning them at all?" Julia was slightly irritated. "What I mean is, why say anything at all if you do not believe them to begin with?" I was beginning to think that discomfort was not a look that suited Blue Dress, as it was obvious that she wished she had not said anything at all.

"As I have said. My cat here, Bubbles, had been acting rather odd. I would like to know the reason for it. Bubbles has never acted like this before, and I would like some explanation for the behavior that did not start until we arrived here."

The hens began to cluck again. Julia was suddenly on the receiving end of advice and old world wisdom. "Well, my dear, I dare say it is because of the new members of the house." A woman in a dreadful hat with birds on it said. This was all beginning to get confusing, and useless to our cause. I looked at Mrs. Winkle, who had come to the middle of the room and was, at present, twining herself through some old crone's legs, rubbing against the woman's hideous blue stockings. The woman absentmindedly picked her up and placed her in her lap, speaking as she did so. "Mrs. Hanson, I understand your concern for your pet. This cat was the only pet of your family for quite some time, I gather. It is only reasonable that it react strangely to any new pets within the household."

Julia considered this for a moment. Eventually, she spoke. "Yes, I suppose that would do it. I just wanted to be sure that there was no other reason for it. I know that cats are very territorial animals, and do not take kindly to new pets in their later years. I suppose that is the explanation, and I thank you for helping me solve this little mystery of mine."

One of the women giggled and said, "My dear, from the size of that cat, I would dare say that the problem was anything but little." At this, the entire group broke into laughter, and Mrs. Winkle and I left. I had been insulted. Not only had they sat about, tossing the one term that I despised the most, they also had the audacity to comment on my size. What it was far too obvious that not many of them had ever missed a meal.

We retreated to the breakfast room, as the women had already toured that part of the house upon their arrival. "Do ya think we should follow 'em?" Mrs. Winkle asked. "Might be one of 'em will say something important." "No, Julia is suspicious as it is. They do not know anything of consequence, and what they do know, they have dismissed as pure rumor." It was disappointing to have come to yet another dead end. If I had only known. "No, Mrs. Winkle, I am sorry to say that we are entirely on our own on this one."

Nigel chose this inopportune moment to stroll in, a look of smug self-satisfaction on his face. "Now, what did I tell you? They knew nothing, and are not ones to tell ghost stories. I knew this would happen. I suppose that now you will drop this silly crusade." I was beyond irate, and I felt I had the right. How dare he make a mockery of this. I had finally had enough, and it was at this moment, I decided if he was not going to keep his opinions to himself, I was going to make the fool of him.

"On the contrary, they knew a great deal about the disturbances. I am sorry to say, however, that no marshmallows were produced. I was quite looking forward to the fireside tales." He looked at me as though I had tread upon his tail. I somewhat like the result. "Do you mock me?" He asked through clenched teeth. "Yes, sir, I mock you. If you are not going to help us, that is your business. However, I suggest you keep your negativity to yourself. We have enough to do without adding your unsolicited attitude to it. I do suggest you curb it, before I am forced to do it for you."

Nigel looked shocked, although he recovered quickly, rearranging his features to look upset. "I am not sure that I know what you mean. I have no attitude. Furthermore, I believe that I told you that you were not going to obtain anything of significance. And from what I gather, you didn't." I had to work to control the growl pent up in my breast. "You are mistaken. However, I do not expect you to understand the significance of what we have found. Now, if you are quite finished, we have work to do."

I made for the door. Nigel, unfortunately, was not about to let it drop. "And just what do you plan on doing? A séance, perhaps?" That was it. I had enough, and I was not about to let this moron have the last word. I spun around as quickly as I could. My huge bulk almost causing me to lose my balance. "Nigel, why don't you just go back to whatever possum hole you have been in? It was far more pleasant when you absented yourself from this situation." This time, I did not wait for him to say anything more. I turned and strode away as fast as I could, Mrs. Winkle hot on my tail. Nigel could be so frustrating, and considering his degree of stubbornness, I thought it best if we avoided him altogether.

My main concern now was the fact that Julia had begun to notice something. I had not intended for the change in my behavior to become so noticeable. It was clear I would have to revert back to routine in order for her to not become more suspicious. It would do no good to have her tailing me. Now I had two problems to contend with. On top of the ghost, I had to find a way to erase any and all of Julia's suspicions. We had derived precious little information from the tea. I felt that we were back to square one. In fact, the meeting had produced far more questions than answers. Who was this Ann Putnam? It is phenomenally frustrating when one cannot simply open a book to gain information. That lack of thumbs again, evolution be hanged!

"Maybe we should go see the barn master. 'Ee knows plenty 'bout this place. 'Ee been 'ere longer than meself and Nigel. Could be 'ee seen somethin' worth the tellin'." Mrs. Winkle made sense. It would stand to reason that he may actually have something to tell us. On the other paw, reason and logic had done a beautiful job of eluding my grasp of late. At that moment, as I stood pondering the wisdom of this course and wondering what good it would do, I hear a hair whitening scream from upstairs.

Chapter Ten

The scream had an unearthly tone to it. It sounded as though it were coming from a different world, and I could feel my fur rising along my spin in response. We scurried out of the kitchen, running as fast as our fat, furry little behinds could go, in the direction of the stairs. At the foot, Nigel joined us, and we three moved up at once. Nigel was naturally faster than either of us, and he reached the landing long before Mrs. Winkle or I were halfway up.

I could see his black tail trailing behind him as he bolted down the corridor at the top of the stairs. When we finally reached the top, we were panting and wheezing from the exertion of so much energy.

I have never agreed with the concept of exercise, however, at the moment, I desperately wish that I did.

"It came from the attic." Nigel said through his panting, his panic almost masked by his exhaustion. The three of us continued, Nigel leading the way. The door to the attic was open, and this, in and of itself, was unusual. Julia had done to a great deal of trouble, explaining to the children that this door was never to be left open. We heard a groan, a low throaty sound that sent shivers through my body. The pause in our movement lasted only a moment, and before I realized it, we were heading up the second set of stairs.

The staircase was long and seemed to go on forever. Eventually, we reached the top, and I could smell the scent of centuries clinging to the boards of the floor. The darkness was disorienting. It took a moment for my eyes to adjust from the gloom. When at last I could see, plumes of disturbed dust swirled through the rays of sunlight that leaked the cracks of the wooden boards that were nailed across the windows. I saw Christine standing in a corner.

Her shoulders were shaking, although, I could not tell if this was from crying, or fear. Her arms were wrapped around her torso in a sort of self hug of reassurance. I could hear the old women and Julia rushing across the lawn, calling out Christine's name.

Her spine was rigid, and I could see the empty boxes that she had brought up lying in a pile at her feet. I began to walk towards her, my paws making obvious tracks in the thick coating of dust that layered the old floor. The sudden action kicked up clouds of it, making the air choking and unbearable.

The old biddies and Julia were rushing up the stairs now. I could hear cheap shoes clicking on the hard wood surface. Julia was hobbling along, her progress slowed by the baby. I don't know how I was registering all of this information, my only conscious thoughts were of Christine. The child may have been old enough to understand several complex concepts, but I just didn't know what a run-in with a ghost would do to her. I twined myself about her legs, looking into her face, searching for a reaction to my presence.

She kept her gaze forward, staring into a dark corner of the room where light gave no comfort. I meowed, attempting to tell her that I was here and she was safe. Still, I received no response. She looked forward, almost as though she could not pull her eyes away from whatever had frightened her. My eyes feel upon what had caused the disruption. I must admit here, dear reader, that I myself was quite taken aback by what I saw.

It was a dressing mannequin, garbed in exactly the same dress our ghost was seen in. The white collar, cuffs, the dark depressing color of the dress. This was it, alright. All that was needed to complete the picture was the white bonnet that would have covered her thick dark hair. I did not understand at first, and while I was getting my thoughts in order, Nigel and Mrs. Winkle simply stayed by the door. I suppose they knew that there was nothing that they could to to aid in this situation. This moment was for Christine and I alone.

The women burst into the room then, enveloping Christine as only mothers and grandmothers can do. I had to back away quickly to avoid the nasty fate of being trampled to death by all those hideous shoes.

They fussed over her, asking questions they would never get an answer to. Embracing Christine, petting her hair, asking what had caused all the commotion.

Even if she would have answered, she could not. They were not allowing her to get a word in edge wise. I could hear Julia waddling up the stairs, panting. I could envision her clutching her swollen belly, trying to get to her daughter. She finally made it to the landing, and the first word from her mouth, "Christine!" belied her concern for her child. She rushed to her as quickly as possible. The effect would have been comical if the situation had been different. Julia wrapped her child in a warm, motherly embrace, forming a shield to keep the bad things out. Stroking the girl's hair, she cooed the words of reassurance that mean the world to every child whom has had a brush with danger.

"Come on, sweetie. What happened? You can tell me. What's wrong, baby?" The women crowded even closer. Their old, wrinkled noses had picked up the scent of juicy gossip. Undoubtedly, they would convene later to discuss it at great length. "For heaven's sake, ladies. My daughter has had a terrible fright. Allow us some room. Chris, what happened? Why did you scream?"

Christine was looking around her, her eyes darting like a caged animal being prepared for slaughter. She did not speak. There were far too many people present for her to feel comfortable enough to relate the tale. Julia was getting impatient. She stood out from Christine at arm's length and took her by the shoulders.

"Now, Chris. I know you have just had the life scared out of you, but how can I help you if you do not tell me what is going on? You have us all a pretty bad start. I think we would all like to know the reason for our early morning run."

Christine did not speak for a moment. Finally, she raised one arm slowly and pointed towards the dark corner of the attic. Julia started, looking back at Christine for some kind of reaction. None came.

Ultimately, she looked in the direction the child was pointing, searching in the darkness. Her gaze fell upon the dress dummy. Looking back at her daughter, as though needing to confirm that this was what had frightened her.

Christine simply stood, her arm raised, one finger protruding, accusing the offensive object. Julia took one more look. Suddenly, the overall expression on her face changed to one of understanding and relief. She began to giggle, the joyful sound filling the room, and seeming altogether out of place in the grimy darkness. At the sound, the women turned, one by one, searching for the cause of this reaction. Finally, they too, saw what had disturbed the child, and they all began to giggle. The giggles soon gave way to outright laughter, and this gave way to something resembling hysterics. This continued for what seemed like a long time. After a piece, everyone calmed down a little, hiccuping and wiping tears from their eyes.

"Oh, honey." Julia said, panting. "It's just an old dress dolly. See, it's just an old dress." She was wiping her eyes with the back of her hand. "That's right, dear. It's just one of the costumes we use for our reenactment week." The woman in the blue dress said. The old hens were digging in their handbags, searching for handkerchiefs to wipe his streaming eyes. The tears were flowing quite freely at this point. As though responding to a signal, the biddies began to move towards the door.

Christine pulled her mother aside. "Wait. Mom, that thing moved. I swear it did." Her eyes were wide. Fear and embarrassment played across the delicate features of her face. Julia sighed in frustration. "Sweetie, it can't move. It's just a dummy wearing a dress." Christine groaned, "Mom, I am not a baby. I know when something can move and when it can't. I am telling you, that thing moved."

Julia was now visibly upset. "Christine, I promise, it can't move. You just saw the wind blowing against it or something." Her daughter tried to say something, but she silenced her. "No, honey. I am telling you that nothing unusual happened here today. Now, I don't want to hear another word about it. After all, we have all been working so hard that I am amazed that the fatigue did not catch up with you until now. Maybe you should go and rest. Then you will see that this was really nothing."

"Mom, I know what I saw. I know that you don't believe in ghosts and all that, but come on. Do you think that I am some little kid that I can't tell what is real and what is not? That thing moved, and on top of that..."

"No, Christine. I don't want to hear another word about it. This is nonsense and you know it. Things do not move about on their own and that is the end of it. Now, we have guests that we must attend to. Come on, help your poor old mother down the stairs."

Christine clammed up, twisting her features into a defiant grimace. She did as she was told and followed her mother down the stairs. At the top, she paused, looking behind her at the dress. Christine's shoulders shook with a powerful, and frightening, shiver before she hurried after her mother.

The next few days passed without incident. Christine passed through them like a wraith, speaking rarely, and sometimes, not at all. She preferred to stay in her room, emerging only for brief periods to eat. It felt as though the girl I knew as Christine was little more than a myth. In her stead was this lethargic, sad creature that now loomed about the household. Her silence was unnerving. She did not read nor go outside, but simply laid upon her bed, not moving from the time she awoke to the time she went to sleep.

The overall feel of the house had changed. Even Toby, whom normally displayed a blatant dislike for his sister, had attempted to draw her out of her shell. Her parents were worried to distraction.

After a time, however, Roger lost all patience with the girl, and made no bones, shall we say, about his anger towards the situation. He wrote it off simply as a mood swing that would eventually pass with time. This only served to further upset Julia, whom had no clue as to what could be upsetting her daughter. "Roger, we cannot treat this lightly. She has never been like this before. I am getting worried."

"Honey, this is nothing, I am telling you. It's going to pass soon, just wait and see." Julia sighed, exasperated that her husband was making this out to be nothing. She had seen what had frightened Christine, and although to her it had not seemed a problem, she knew that it had something to do with her daughter's behavior now. "Seriously, Jules. Are you telling me that you didn't have mood swings when you were growing up? "No, but mine never lasted this long. I want to take her to see a doctor. Maybe he will be able to tell us why she is acting like this."

"Darling, I will not have this town gossiping about how my child has lost her mind. Oh, I know she hasn't, but that's what they will be saying. We only just got here. Something like this could jeopardize my career."

Julia rolled her eyes and threw up her hands.

"So, your career is more important than your daughter's health. I can't believe that I am hearing you say this. I never thought that furthering your career would ever be put above your family."

"Julia, don't overreact. I am not saying I am not worried about Christine. I am. It's just that if we made a fuss like this every time she had one of her moods, that's all we would do. I just think that we should wait a little longer before we go making any rash decisions."

I was growing quite tired of listening to this debate. I was weary of Julia and Roger not doing what they should be. They should have been listening to their daughter and comprehending what she had to say rather than replaying this discussion and writing off what had frightened her as frivolous. I decided that if they were just going to sit and do nothing about it, I would. As I headed up the stairs, I had a few moments to reflect upon what I had heard thus far of her experience. A part of me believed her story. I wondered what she had seen, as it was quite obvious that the question was not had she seen anything, but what? A small portion of me hoped that she had really seen nothing more than the dress dummy and she had been startled, her imagination conjuring up a suitable image. I had originally set out to discover the source of all this to prevent such a situation from arising. I had failed my family by not stopping this. My Christine had paid the price for my negligence. It was not my responsibility to aid her in her hour of need.

Christine was, predictably, in her room, laying face down across her bed. The air was heavy with her melancholy. I padded softly to the bed. Looking up, I could only see her feet dangling over the edge. I jumped, with a certain air of grace and poise I might add, joining her. She did not stir, even though my leap of faith had caused the mattress to shift noticeably. It was at this moment that I understood how great her distress was. I flicked my tail over her bare ankles, and again, I was not granted a response.

I was beginning to get a bit frustrated. There had never been a problem that I had been unable to help her with. I moved farther along, in hopes this would jolt her out of the trance that was consuming her. It did not. I walked around in front of her, deciding that she could not ignore me if I was literally in her face. Nuzzling her face with my nose, I purred as I did so. This was an attempt to inform her that I was here and I could comfort her.

To my delight, she lifted one arm slowly and began to stroke my back. I lay down beside her, and she rolled to her side, propping her head on one hand as she did so. She sighed, a painful sound that spoke volumes about her current emotional state.

"It's not fair, Bubbles." Her tone was unlike anything I had ever heard. Raw, and emotional. "They see you acting all crazy and the whole world has to stop to find out what's wrong with you. I see one strange thing and I get yelled at for imagining things." The poor child. She really had seen something that shook her to her very core. At this moment, I felt that it was a pity that humans would not understand that felines are capable of speech. I desperately wished that I could tell Christine everything that I knew. She needed someone to believe her right now, and I wanted to tell her that I did. I nudged her under the chin, purring loudly.

"It's not like I have lost my mind or anything. I really did see it. I know that mom and dad don't believe me, but I did. And it was scary. I mean, I know that things like that can't move on their own. I'm not a baby. But, if mom had seen it, she would have freaked out like I did."

She sighed again and rolled on to her back. Putting one arm behind her head, she stared up at the ceiling for a few more minutes before she spoke again. "I mean, mom did tell me to put all the empty boxes in the attic. I had just finished putting all my stuff away, and I wanted to get rid of those boxes.

They made my room look ugly. So, I took them upstairs. I got a weird feeling on my back, like a tingle or something. I don't know what it was, but I turned around to see if someone was behind me. I couldn't see at first, it's really dark up there. It took me a minute to make out the outline of the dress. I thought it was pretty cool to find something like that up there. I thought maybe if it was the right size, I could wear it for Halloween. I touched the sleeve, the material was really rough. I heard something. It sounded like a door being opened on squeaky hinges. I backed away from the dress real quick. I thought Toby was bringing boxes from his room and I was going to help him. No one came up. So, when I looked back at the dress, there was someone in it. There were hands coming out of the sleeves. I thought I must be seeing thing, I think I even shook my head to clear my eyes or something."

She paused for a moment, folding her hands across her stomach. "I've thought about it a hundred times. I know what I saw! Just thinking about it gives me the creeps."

Christine rolled to her side so quickly, it made me jump. She was facing me now and the look in her eyes told me she was desperate to get whatever it was that she had to say out and into the world to make it work. To make it real. "I know I can trust you, Bubbles. You don't think I'm crazy. I'll tell you what I saw next. That dress, well, there was a girl in it!"

Chapter Eleven

" I don't know who she was. She was very pretty. No makeup, and her hair was dark and tucked under this cute little white bonnet. Dark eyes. She didn't scare me. I've seen all those old horror movies, and once you get used to them, it's hard to get scared at anything like that. What scared me is what happened next."

Christine paused, swallowing hard. I could understand her trepidation in finishing. "She lifted one of her arms and pointed at me. She had a funny look. I don't know what you would call it. Accusing, I guess? She started to scream, but nothing came out of her mouth. No sound. Nothing. She was tearing at her hair and her arms were flailing around. She looked crazy or possessed or something. That's when I screamed."

She rolled onto her stomach again, folding her hands under her chin. "She was there, Bubbles. I know she was. When I screamed, she disappeared.

Just vanished, right there in front of me. I wish someone would believe me."

I do, Christine, I believe you. She looked at me then, cocking her head to one side. "You do, don't you, Bubbles? You know I saw something. I know you have seen some weird stuff around here too. I just wish you could tell mom and dad to believe me too." I nuzzled her chin again. I wanted her to know that I did, in fact, believe her.

I walked down the stairs. My resolve was only strengthened by what I had just learned from Christine. I was not going to allow the family to be involved any further. In fact, I could not understand why the spirit had brought Christine into this in the first place. I had to get to the bottom of this, no matter what that entailed.

Perhaps if I could act quickly enough, in time, Christine would believe that she had never really seen anything at all. In my opinion, it was bad enough that these things were happening to begin with, but now I was truly furious. If I knew how, I might have located the ghost and given her a piece of my mind.

I headed toward the parlor. I needed time to think, to sort this all out. Having no desire to speak with anyone, I needed solitude. Julia had the good taste to place two long, wooden benches beneath the windows in this room. Topped with overstuffed cushions, this would be the ideal place to organize my thoughts and subsequent actions. I lay down, the warm sunlight giving me an odd sense of comfort that dispersed as quickly as it had came. I could not allow myself to feel comfort, not with all that had happened. I fervently wished that I had followed my feline instinct and done something, anything, to prevent our coming here. This was all on my shoulders. I had failed my family.

Since the frightful episode in the attic, Nigel and Mrs. Winkle had let me alone. I had not seen a single strand of fur of them since we had left the attic on that day. I felt that this was somewhat fortuitous, as I had needed that time to sort things out. I had yet to come to any real conclusions on the subject, and I felt that this was never going to be over until I did something myself to bring it to an end.

Now that I had been made painfully aware of all that had transpired in the attic, I felt that another opinion on the subject might be valuable. Perhaps from there, I could deduce a rough theory as to just what was going on in this house. In retrospect, perhaps I should have sought out my fellow felines. I was not yet ready, unfortunately, to hold a council until I could decide upon a theory as to why Christine had an experience. I went to the study. Having never taken the time to inspect the room completely, I felt that I might be able to mull my thoughts about while I checked things over. I began to inspect the bookshelves. I had been far too preoccupied to ensure that the unpacking had been properly accomplished. I wanted to be sure that my absence had not caused any harm. I was admiring the way that Julia's favorite books seemed to belong here. As though these very shelves had been designed with her extensive collection in mind.

I heard someone whistling, a rather welcome sound, as the overall atmosphere of the house as of late had been one of sorrow and misunderstanding. The tune was cheerful, coming from the soul. As though the lips that it was issued from belonged to a person who could not be anything but grateful for simply being alive on this day in this space.

Perhaps Roger was out in the yard. He often whistled while he worked, taking very seriously the philosophy presented by Mr. Walt Disney in the 1930's.

It was at this moment that I realized that the sound was not coming from outside, but the very interior of this room. Looking to my right, I discovered the source of this happy melody.

In the corner, happily dusting away with a teeny rag, was dear little Roscoe. He was whistling his teeny, tiny heart out, as though he could not imagine a better place to be than right where he was. The realization came upon me that the house never seemed to need a good scrubbing, and here was the reason. While the humans took care of the larger chores, the various creatures on the property handled the details.

Somehow, this revelation made me more depressed than when I had entered. Not only had I failed to protect the family, I was not lifting a paw to aid in the daily operations of the house. During my little kitty pity part, Roscoe's fat mousy rump was swinging in time to his tune.

"Good day, Roscoe." I said gently, doing my best not to startle him. The memory of our first meeting flooded my mind, and if it were possible to give myself a swift kick in my own rump, I would have done so. Hard. Roscoe turned, "Oh, hello there, Bubbles. Didn't here you come in. Haven't seen you around much lately." He continued with his task, humming softly.

"Well, Christine had a rather bad time the other day, and I have been trying to sort it out." He stopped what he was doing and turned so suddenly that it almost caused him to fall over. "What do you mean, a bad time?" "It is a bit difficult to explain. I would hardly know where to begin. You see, she believes that she saw something unusual. What I am attempting to sort out is if she truly did, see something, that is. If so, than why?" I saw no harm in telling him all of this. I needed to talk to someone, and somehow, I knew that Roscoe would take me seriously. He struck me as a rather level-headed fellow, and it would be nice to get a second opinion. Nothing, absolutely nothing, could have prepared me for what he said next. "So, she had a meeting with our ghost? What's so unusual about that? Why should Christine not see her? It makes perfect sense if you stop and think about it for a minute."

He waved one chubby little paw about, as though this gesture effectively dismissed the subject. In my humble opinion, the subject would most certainly was not dismissed. "How could you say that makes perfect sense? I have considered every possibility and I have yet to come to a sensible conclusion. I think that it is most unusual. Christine has nothing at all to do with any of this, so why should she have seen anything to begin with?" Roscoe gave me the soft look of one who was dealing with a simpleton. "What I mean to say is, of course our little spirit friend would make herself known to the child. I mean, they are practically the same age!"

Chapter Twelve

I was quite taken aback by Roscoe's logic. For a moment, I was far too stunned to speak. He stared at me, studying my reaction. I am sure that my expression was one of disbelief. "What's the matter? Don't think it makes any sense, do you?" "On the contrary, my good mouse, it makes a bit too much sense for comfort. It would stand to reason Christine would and could have something to do with this. Yet, I am still disinclined to put all of my hopes on that alone. I wonder, though, if that were the answer to all of this, why would the ghost have waited until now to reveal her presence to Christine? After all, we have been here long enough for this to have occurred much sooner if that were the case."

Roscoe's lip curled in frustration and disgust. He was obviously displeased with me. "Look, mate, I can't solve everything for you. All I know is what I see. I see that the ghost and our little lady appear to be the same age. Seems to me that might be something worth lookin' into."

I did not completely understand, but he did present an interesting theory. While our conversation did present a new point to ponder, it seemed to me that there was far more to all of this than just Christine. If anything, my little chat with Roscoe had, not surprisingly, produced far more confusion than clarity.

I wandered from the study. The dizzy feeling in my head resembled the time I was involved in a feline fight and I was punch drunk for a few days. I was lost so deeply in my thoughts, I honestly had no idea where I was going. I found myself on the back porch, right after running head first into the door jam. That will teach me to walk and think at the same time.

I was jolted back to reality, having been blinded by the harsh sunlight. Toby was off to my right, kicking a soccer ball in between two trees that he had apparently appointed as temporary goal posts.

Digger had been quite busy, the evidence showing in the neatly tilled flower beds and the scent of damp earth that clung to the morning air. I went to the steps and sat down, taking this moment to father my thoughts. It was a difficult task considering the precious little information that I had. Suddenly, it dawned on me that I needed to know far more than I did. The trouble with this was that I needed more strange occurrences in order to gain the information that I so desperately needed. This, of course, had the potential for disaster.

Sometime later, I prowled beneath the table in the breakfast nook. This had become something of the family dining area, as the dining room itself was deemed to formal for daily use. As the family dined on sandwiches, my mind was consumed with the turmoil that had gripped the household of late. I dared not abandon my regular duties. The disposal of scraps was central to my position in the house, and I did not wish for my authority to be impugned simply because I failed to attend to my duties. After all, one's tummy does not stop growling simply because one is on a mission. I had to keep up my strength for the task at hand.

As a result of our conversation, it seemed as though Christine had become comfortable enough to resume her normal routine. Julia was up there, gushing about how pleased she was that the child was growing up and effectively abandoning the world of fantasy. Julia believed that the little episode in the attic was ridiculous, and was quite content that her daughter had apparently realized this for herself.

I could see Christine's legs wriggling about under the table, communicating her discomfort with the topic of conversation. Hearing a sound behind me, I turned. It quite resembled air escaping from a tire. To my surprise, I spied Nigel peering around the kitchen island. He gestured with his head that he had some important news to share with me. Jerking his head quickly to one side, he crept from the room, and I followed. If only because I was anxious to relieve myself of the dark mood that had consumed me of late. We entered the foyer where Mrs. Winkle awaited us. I smiled, happy to see my friend again.

"Well, 'ello there, poppet." I hadn't realized until that moment how much I had missed her companionship. I nuzzled her nose with mine, wishing that words could describe how deeply I had felt her absence. Nigel took command immediately. Conveying his annoyance in his tone, he seemed to forget that, for the moment, I was merely tolerating his presence. Another head was needed on this situation, and my choices were limited. "Now, now. This in no time for a tearful reunion. We must decide what to do next. We simply cannot allow the family to continue to be involved to this degree. Bubbles, whilst you have been in your own little world, we have been doing some investigating. Perhaps you would like to hear of our finding, provided that you are now properly prepared for it, of course."

It sounded very much like he was implying that I had been having something of a kitty hissy fit. On the whole, I resented it. However, since Nigel had finally decided that this was, in fact serious, and had pulled himself out of his own emotional rut, I decided to let the comments slide.

"Why, Nigel. I am glad that you have decided that the situation is unacceptable. Yet, I wonder at your renewed vigor in solving this mystery."

I purposely sounded condescending, for no other reason than to merely irritate him. I was annoyed that it had taken the attic to jolt him enough to become involved. Nigel ignored me, and instead, forged ahead in his narration.

"We have spoken to the barn master, a Mr. Tibbs. He was a wealth of information that we believe could be quite useful. Unfortunately, we can draw no solid conclusions based on this new information, or even how it pertains to our current dilemma. We were of the mind that perhaps you could aid us."

"Well, I will help if I can, of course. I do not, however, understand how you are unable to draw any conclusions. Mrs. Winkle knows as much as I. As such, I do not see where I may have anything new to offer."

This was all very confusing. "Well, ducky, it's like this. From what you told me 'bout what the ghost showed you, you know more than we do. We can't make no sense of it, you see. Don't know what to do know. 's difficult to explain it is." Nigel was giving Mrs. Winkle a look that effectively communicated the silent message of "Shut up!"

"Listen to me, Bubbles," he said, "as it is, we would like you to hear this from the barn master himself. Straight from the horse's mouth, if you will pardon the pun." He snorted at his own wit, and I cringed at the infamous dry British humor.

I thought it best to move on with the topic at hand, considering the suggestion for a moment.

My singular experience with the apparition had been frightening enough, and I had gathered from jimmy that the barn master was not exactly the most loveable of folk. As such, I was not thrilled at the prospect of having to meet him. A monster of Jimmy's size that possessed a surly disposition did nothing to raise my spirits. The image of being trampled by one of those enormous hooves flashed before me, and I did my best to push it out of my mind. Not because it seemed silly, mind you. It was merely for the simple reason that if I lingered too long on the image of my generous physique spread out all the more as a result of a good and thorough stomping, I would lose any nerve I could possibly muster.

"All right, Nigel," I said, "We will go to see the barn master. I am just as anxious as yourself, if not more so, to get to the bottom of this." Mrs. Winkle chose this moment to pipe in with her two bits. "See there, I told you our little poppet wouldn't let us down. Stout 'eart 'ee 'as." Nigel rolled his eyes as if to say, "Why must I be cursed with this simpleminded twit?"

I resented his disdain. Mrs. Winkle had been a constant companion and had proven herself a true friend. Surely, an elder of the felines deserved far more respect than this pompous snob was showing her. Add to that the mere fact that Mrs. Winkle was tougher than claws, and I had come to the conclusion that there was far more to her then met the eye.

"I suggest we make haste. We will not benefit from further incident, and any knowledge that can be obtained from Mr. Tibbs might come to be useful should the spirit return." I wished that Nigel would acknowledge, if not my blatant superiority, at least the fact that, at this point, I knew more than he. I did not think myself above him, often. Rather, I had had far more luck than he with our specter, and I could very well handle things. Now, if only I could point out to him that he did not need to assert himself to the point of nausea. I am sure that the fact that the ghost chose myself and not he for her communication lent fuel to the fire of his jealousy. His belligerent attitude was becoming quite tiresome, and all I wished was to yawn in his face. Kitty breath and all.

"I presume that you will wish to act as something of a commander in chief for this, shall we say, expedition?" Nigel was calm, and had it not been for the fluffing of his tail, a sure signal of irritation in a feline, I might have been a bit more friendly. That is the trouble with being a member of the feline race. While our tone can be cool and calm, our tail, or some other portion of our anatomy, belies our true feelings. As such, we are not very accomplished when it comes to the refined skill of lying. I often admire humans, for they have no portion of their bodies that betray their true feelings. I sometimes feel it a pity that such an admirable quality is wasted upon the poor, weak souls.

"Nigel, it would be nothing if not disastrous should we neglect to work together on this. I have no desire to appoint a chain of command. In fact, I do believe that a truce is in order, temporary or otherwise. It could prove to be beneficial for all concerned, don't you agree?" He bore a look about his face that very much resembled the expression of one whom possessed a hair ball. The overall effect was quite comical, if I do say so, and I immensely enjoyed the rare moment of speechlessness that had overtaken him. Seeing as these moments are quite rare in Nigel's presence, I savored the relief that passed over me while he attempted, in vain, to regain his composure. I wasted to time in taking advantage of the temporary pause, and turned to Mrs. Winkle.

"What exactly did the barn master say?"

I seemed to be having the effect of surprise on all around me, for it took a second for her to respond. "Well, it's like I said. We think you should 'ear it from 'im, we do. Wouldn't make a bit o' sense if meself were to try and explain it. When I do try, the words get all jumbled like, and they don't come out right."

This elder feline amazed me so. One moment, she would be tough and unyielding, and the next, she was wringing her paws in worry. She was as enigmatic as our current dilemma, if not more so.

"In that case, I suggest that we go and see the barn master. If I need to know what new evidence he possesses, and you two are obviously not going to tell me anything, then I should like to hear what he has to say." I glared at Nigel, whom seemed to have recovered from his temporary paralysis. He, in turn, gave a decisive nod of his head.

"That is precisely what we had intended all along. No sense in wasting more time than we already have."

I began to head for the door, and they followed suit. Nigel said not a word. I suppose he had decided that it was best to allow a small victory, unchallenged. We walked to the barn in relative silence. I could hear Digger off in the distance somewhere, going about his business. For a brief moment, I envied him so, wishing that I, too, could be as untouched as he.

Our walk was so silent that I was briefly amazed at Nigel's apparent ability to be quiet for more than a brief second. Unfortunately, the blessed moment of silence was not to endure. I could hear Jimmy and the others scattered through the fenced in pasture. We stopped at a large wooden fence. Nigel leapt to the top of the post, once again showing that he was trimmer than myself and able to accomplish tasks that I despise, no matter the reading on the scale. He waited a few moment, searching the flat green land with his gaze. He must have finally spotted his quarry, and called out, "Mr. Tibbs, could we have a moment of your time?"

I heard a snort that seemed to convey the impatience of the poor animal. The sound of hoof beats filled the air. I envisioned a beast of Jimmy's size and stature, or perhaps even larger, as I could see no other way one could control these monsters.

What paused before us struck me dumb. I had been expecting a large, beast of a creature, a force to be reckoned with. Not quite. I doubt this thing could have been taller than Toby. Roger could break this thing in half should he have had the gall to attempt to mount it. I, with my large, voluminous body, could have jumped over this thing without my legs so much as grazing it's back. I had to hold up my paw to suppress a laugh. I was tickled by the idea that Jimmy was afraid of this creature when he quite easily could have stomped it into the ground.

"Haven't you bothered me enough already? Now, Nigel, you know I don't have time for this. I gotta keep a close watch on all these ninnies. It don't do me a bit of good to leave them on their own. Before you know it, their into the oats and there be none left for supper." Mr. Tibbs voice was low and gruff. And very out of breath. And very annoyed.

"Yes, yes, I know, Mr. Tibbs. I do apologize for the inconvenience. However, we do need to trouble you just once more, for the benefit of Bubbles here. After that, we shall be on our way."

There was a moment of tense silence as Mr. Tibbs looked me over. I suppose this was to determine whether or not I was worth the bother. I must say, what Mr. Tibbs lacked in size, he certainly made up for in charisma. He had a, shall we say, air about him that made it easy to understand how he could run herd on such brutes.

"Why do you need to waste my time with this again?" The impatience was very clear. "I've already told you once, why don't you just tell it and leave me alone to my duties?"

He was prancing about restlessly, back and forth, his head swinging from side to side in a gesture of frustration. This was a horse with far better things to do than stand about conversing with three felines. This topped me off that what he had to say was very important indeed. You see, when someone has something important to tell, they prefer to tell it once. The mere fact that he did not wish to discuss it again was proof that he was telling the truth. Liars often state things more than once, to convince their listeners they are being honest. As though, through repetition, fiction becomes truth.

Unfortunately, I was beginning to feel rather guilty that I had not forced the information out of Nigel and Mrs. Winkle, opting, instead, to infringe upon Mr. Tibbs' time. "My dear Mr. Tibbs," Nigel broke in, "I am sure that you could tell it far better than either of us. After all, if I were to attempt it, I am quite sure that it would come out all wrong. That would not do you any justice, now would it?" Nigel was entreating upon his ego. Somehow, it seemed to be working.

He sighed, "Well, I guess I could take a few minutes." He conceded, "But this is the last time. I got things to do, and I can't be bothered all the time just cause you fuzz heads can't get it right." He glanced out to pasture. "Meet me in the barn. I'll be there after I check on these boys." I looked about the barn as we waited. My last visit had been unintentional and rushed. As a result, I had no real opportunity to look about. I was surprised to see that it was quite orderly. Freshly swept, with the scent of clean straw throughout. This place had a rather comfortable feel about it. The occupants were clearly happy to be here.

We sat upon the edge of a wooden trough, the same that Jimmy had told me to drink from to regain my composure. The memory of that brief meeting caused me to smile. Never had I been so privileged to know someone so straightforward and honest."Alright, I need to make this quick." Mr. Tibbs rushed in. "Now, Bubbles!" I snapped to attention.

The tone of his voice was very imposing. I got the feeling that what was about to be said was very grave indeed, and I did not wish to miss a word of it. The look in his eyes sent a shiver down my spine, and I could tell that he was still shaken by whatever it was that he had to tell me.

"Now, I was told by Mrs. Winkle and Nigel here that you done seen our ghost." I nodded my assent on cue, and he continued. "Well, I don't want this getting' around, but, uh," His gaze darted about wildly, and I had a fairly good idea of what was about to be said. He cleared his throat and shook his head, as though he could not believe that he was about to say this to a mere feline. Suddenly, he blurted out, "I done seen her too!" He paused dramatically, and I gave the proper gasp of shock to show that not only was I listening, but I was also astonished.

"I know, I'm not the type to believe in fairy tales and spook stories and all. But I swear on my saddle that I done seen her. It was a none too good thing, neither. Scared me halfway out of my saddle blanket." I was doing my best to stay interested in all of this rambling. Unfortunately, I had predicted this and was little more than underwhelmed. Mr. Tibbs took offense to this. "Look here, you little fuzz ball. I really did see her. It was late one night, after all the boys were supposed to be back in the barn. I was makin' my rounds. See, they likes to sneak out every now and then for a late night graze, and I had to make sure they was where they was supposed to be. Well, I was out by the north fence," He nodded his head in the proper direction.

"And I was walkin' around, minding my own bidness, when I heard a noise. A creakin' I guess you could call it."

At that, I looked at Mrs. Winkle. We, too, had heard a creaking sound just before the apparitions had appeared. She nodded, and I turned back to Mr. Tibbs, whom was obviously annoyed that I was not paying rapt attention.

"Well, I started to walk over to the tree near the fence. See, sometimes tree branches make that kinda noise just when theys about to break. So, I just wanted to know if I needed to tell Digger he had an extra chore in the mornin'. I was comin' round the tree, and I see a pair of dark boots, danglin' in my face. And them boots, well, they was attached to a pair of legs. And that pair of legs was attached to a body. That body was attached to a neck, and that neck was swingin' from the tree with a piece of rope!"

Chapter Thirteen

"Don't know who she coulda been. I could see a bit a grayin' in her hair, so's my guess is she had seen a few winters in her day. Well, I will tell you, that part of it, it scared me enough, it surely did." Mr. Tibbs stopped and gulped several times against what could only have been the proverbial lump that had settled in his throat. His eyes were darting back and forth in a panicked frenzy. This gesture only served to bring the indignation that was welling up within me to the boiling point.

"That part of it?" I asked, my voice reaching the pitch of caterwaul. "You mean to tell me there is more to this?"

Mr. Tibbs leveled his gaze at me, glaring pointedly. His enormous brown eyes searing any frustration I had previously felt to a small pile of ashes, leaving me feeling very foolish indeed. "If you would kindly shut it!" His gaze was fixed upon me, effectively letting me know that if I did not keep my furry trap closed, he would show me what the business end of a hoof looked like, up close and personal.

"I will be most happy to explain," He said, the words dripping with disdain. "There was more to it, as though I hadn't already been through enough.

No, it was just my luck that there was more to come. What happened next was enough to convince me that I don't know nothin' 'bout nothin'." He was building up to the climax of the tale. Beating the proverbial horse to death, if you will pardon the pun. I was becoming quite irritated at his overdrawn sense of dramatics. I sighed a little, hoping this would implore him to continue his tale. I am unaware if this is what compelled him to do my silent bidding, or if he had simply run out of things to say that, in essence, said nothing.

"I was standing there, starin' at this horrid sight, when all a sudden, I heard a rusteling sound. Like when you be walkin' through grass, you know that soft sort of swish? It was comin' from around the other side of the tree, so I figured I might take a look. Now, I tell you, right then, I was the most scared I ever been in my life. I was hopin' that it was just one of my boys, out for a midnight graze. Lord, woulda given my right hoof if that was it, hell, all of 'em. But somethin' told me this was far from over." I had correctly predicted what was to be said thus far. I had deduced that Mr. Tibbs had an experience similar to mine. I was a bit afraid to hear the remainder of this.

"Around the tree came another girl, younger, very pretty from my reckonin'. Myself, I prefer a chestnut mare with a long flowin' mane,..." He stared off for a moment, as though his beloved were standing before him. I practically had to cough up a hairball to get his attention.

"Oh, sorry." I was unaware that a horse could look so sheepish. "Now, where was I? Oh, yes, the girl. She was real calm like, as though she had seen bodies swingin' from trees her whole life." But, she did, I thought to myself. "She was lookin' up at the hanged woman. Well, I don't know what got under her saddle, but suddenly, she started actin' real crazy like. She was clawin' at her hair, screamin' like the devil was in her. I mean, she scared the hell outta me! She was pointin' at the hanged lady and grabbin' at her throat, runnin' her fingernails down her face and leavin' deep red cuts that were just oozin' blood. This poor girl was just off her rocker, if you know what I mean. Well, I just got so nervous; I lit outta there fast as my teeny legs could carry me. Trust me, an Arabian couldn'ta beat me to the finish line that time."

It was quite apparent that the simple act of relating his ordeal brought the panic that he felt at that moment to the surface all over again.

The poor creature looked as though he were ready to bold at that moment.

Now, how did I fit into all of this? Certainly, it was interesting, but I did not see why Nigel had been so insistent that I hear this from Mr. Tibbs. Surely he could have told me all this, and spared the barn master any further embarrassment.

The most disturbing aspect of all this was that we added a second apparition to our current dilemma. I wondered for perhaps the umpteenth time, just what had we gotten into?

Suddenly, I realized that the three of them were staring at me. It was clear that they believed I held all the answers, and wondering why I was not sharing them. I was about to say that I was overwhelmed, but that would have been an understatement of epic proportions.

"Well, what do ya 'ave ter say 'bout all this?" Mrs. Winkle peered at me with her sharp eyes. "Truth be told, I haven't the foggiest on what to say. I do not see why this should have anything to do with me. Further, I have no idea why you and Nigel couldn't have simply told me this. It would have saved Mr. Tibbs valuable time."

"Now, I don't know why I wasted my time talkin' to yer snooty little fur ball here. I am a busy pony, I don't have time for this!" I had upset him, and had not meant to. "Mr. Tibbs, please, I meant no offense. Suffice to say that we could have saved us all a good deal of everything had these two simply told me your story instead of dragging yourself and I out here for a clandestine conference."

I was more than confused. I was completely clueless as to what to do from here. I was growing rather weary of the cloaks and dagger approach to all this. I felt that direct logic would be best, as we could go through a process of elimination.

Mr. Tibbs shook his head. "Well, I have to agree with ya there. But, done is done. No help for it now. Anyway, there it is. I hope it's helpful."

"I am sure it is." I said. I must admit, I didn't know how helpful it would be as of yet, but I had no idea what would come next.

"I am glad to hear that. I gotta say, it's awful nice to know that I wasn't going off my rocker. Up to now, I just though I had mixed a little too much barley with the hops at feeding time." He snorted, rearing his head towards the door. "Now, I think it's time that ya'll got outta here. They'll be back soon, and I have work to do." "We understand completely. I do wish there was someone who would help us make sense of all this. I must admit, there is very little I am able to comprehend these days." "You could always go to see Madam Luna. Could be she may be able to help." Mr. Tibbs offered.

Nigel clicked his tongue. "That mad woman?"

He said, "I doubt she would be able to offer us anything useful." "You don't hafta go!" Mr. Tibbs growled, "I was only trying to help."

I broke in. "I am sure that it is sound advice, and I will go to see her, even if Nigel will not." I glared at him, wondering why he had chosen that time to speak as he did.

We took our leave of the barn master. As we walked back to the house, I was confused. How was all of this connected? True, the sightings all had the same elements, yet, I was unable to find a common thread that we could use to put all of the pieces together and put an end to it.

Chapter Fourteen

I awoke the next morning, feeling very stiff indeed. The previous evening had yielded few results. We had returned from the barn, and I had worked up the courage to ask Nigel about Madam Luna and why he had scoffed so when her name had been mentioned.

Nigel had simply called her a few choice phrases and left to the kitchen in a huff. As I stretched, I could hear the sounds of the family coming to life. Soon, there would be breakfast, followed by a round of shopping for Julia and the kids while Roger went to the office. Julia had in mind to purchase a crib today and have it set up when Roger returned that evening.

I trotted downstairs to await the arrival of my morning meal and perhaps have a chance to speak with Mrs. Winkle without Nigel's interference. Unfortunately, this was not to be.

He was already in attendance when I arrived. My frustration grew when he stopped mid-sentence. I wondered if he would ever cease to be a nuisance and began to be helpful.

"Please, do not allow me to interrupt. Continue, I will be happy to wait." I said as graciously as I could at this hour of the morning with an empty stomach. "I was just telling Mrs. Winkle that we should get an early start this morning. It is a rather long walk to Madam Luna's" Nigel said, "We were debating as to whether or not to wake you."

I must say, my jaw hit the floor. Here was Nigel, endorsing the very idea that he had so openly scoffed at the evening before. "You don't say." I responded. "Well, I suggest that we dine first. If it is to be a long journey then we shall need to be at our best, don't you agree?"

Once we had feasted, we set out. It was indeed a long walk to Madam Luna's residence. After a time, we came upon a rather ramshackle dwelling in a terrible state of disrepair. It was a log cabin that crouched among a small cluster of trees. It put me in mind of an old guard dog, far past it's prime, and yet, still ready to attack.

As we drew closer, I could detect a strange odor upon the breeze. Not completely disagreeable, yet bitter at the back of the throat. A faint curl of smoke rose from within, emanating from the chimney, or what was left of it at any rate. An ominous feeling came over me, as though this would prove to be a useful experience on our quest for the truth. No light came from within. We could hear faint, rhythmic mutterings from inside. The fur along my spine stood at attention then, and I did not like the sensation that were causing this reaction.

"Come in." A rather scratchy voice said. "I have been expecting you." I glanced at my companions. They looked as perturbed as I, and yet, I was resolved to see this through. Gathering my calm, we pressed inside.

Here, the odor was more potent, and I could feel it seeping into my every pore. To this day, I swear I catch a faint whiff of it from time to time. As my vision adjusted to the darkness, I was able to make out that this was a one room shack. A fireplace at the back, directly opposite the door, small shelves lining the wall to my right. A small cauldron stood at the center of the room, faint wisps of flame licking from beneath. I could see a figure crouching near the cauldron, barely distinguishable as that of a feline. Her fur was black as ink. So deep and rick that if one stared long enough, one could see the stars of the sky hidden deep within. Her eyes were a piercing blue, and had the look of ages behind them. Why, they looked as though they had gazed upon the fall of Rome itself!

"Come closer, dearies. I mean ye no harm." The voice said again, though I could swear that her lips moved not at all. I opened my mouth to explain the reason behind our intrusion when she silenced me with a gesture. "No need. I know why you have come."

Needless to say, I was rendered quite speechless. An unusual condition for myself, I assure you. We crept a slight bit closer and seated ourselves. "I know what it is that you seek." She said.

"Oh, Really!" Nigel broke in. "Are the commonplace theatrics really necessary? For the love of Pete, Oriana, get on with it!" "Now, Nigel, was that polite?" Mrs. Winkle asked under her breath. She nudged him slightly, as if to continue scolding him without saying it.

"Never mind, Mrs. Winkle." Madam Luna spoke up, a honeyed voice emanating in place of the throaty sound. "You do not know Nigel as I do."

For the second time in as many minutes, I was stunned beyond verbal capability. Thus far, Madam Luna was all an act, a sham. I suddenly began to wonder at the wisdom of seeking her advice. "Now, Nigel. You know that I am bound by custom and tradition." Madam Luna scolded. Nigel appeared kittenish, as though his mum were berating him for taking the last bit of tuna.

"Very well, have it your way. You!" She pointed at me. "You are the cause of all of this. It is you who have brought back these spirits in full force." "Me?" I squeaked, not comprehending my role in any of this nonsense. "And how, pray thee, is that." "Shut yer trap and I'll tell you." She snapped. "You are the catalyst by which these events came to pass. You have a direct link to these events running through your blood. Why else would you succeed where Nigel has failed so miserably?"

What in Bast's name was she going on about? I have a blood link? Impossible! "Not so impossible when you consider the mating of felines, my dear." She moved towards a shelf, dragging a leather bound book towards the flames with her teeth. "I will show you what I mean. Look here." She turned the pages. "This is a complete blood history of every feline in our clan, spanning the ages from the time of 1693. Do you know what occurred in that year?"

I searched my brain for a moment, caught quite off guard by this sudden pop quiz of feline history. A subject I have never really cared for.

"That was a dark time. A time when human history turned its deepest shade of black. The witch trials of Salem Towne." She paused for dramatic emphasis. "Yes, a dark time indeed.

Many of the people were tried for meaningless things. Many were innocent of the crimes they were charged with. One victim has been passed over and forgotten, lost to history. This innocent soul had done nothing. Indeed, he was not even accused formally. The townsfolk were so caught up in their hysteria, they murdered this poor soul without even the excuse of a guilty verdict."

"Do not misunderstand me, Madam," I said, unaware that the information about to be given to me would change my life. "But, how do I fit into all of this?" "I am getting to that, oh impatient one." Madam Luna rolled her eyes, unable to contain her disgust at my interruption. "This victim was no ordinary being. Oh, no. He was far more than that. He was Samuel Goode's beloved pet, Lasater. Murdered, no, sacrificed to the gods of mob rule over three hundred years ago. The townspeople believed that Lasater was Sarah Goode, Samuel's mother, come back from the grave. In their minds, they needed to destroy him to stop the cycle of witchcraft. Little

did they know of the truth."

"And that being?" I asked, anxious to hear the end of this. "That being that Lasater was a guardian. He was there to protect Samuel and his family from the mob's endless fury and stupidity. Samuel was only a young boy at the time of his mother's murder and Lasater came to bring comfort and security. This was stolen from Samuel on the day of Lasater's death. Little did he know that Lasater had bred extensively among the female felines of the village, thus providing many heirs to take on his responsibility."

"For pity's sake, Oriana, get to the point!" Nigel grumbled, his impatience radiating throughout the room. "This is fine storytelling for the campfire, but I do not see how this has any bearing on our current situation."

"You old fool!" Madam Luna's voice boomed throughout the room. "You know nothing of sacred things, and now you tell me to get to the point."

She rose upon her hind legs, standing erect as humans do. "This is not for you! You have nothing to do with this, and that is why you failed. Are you so blind? Can you not see that the occurrences have grown in number since Bubbles' arrival. Do you not know what that means?" Nigel shrank under her glare, as though he were trying to creep beneath the floorboards to escape her wrath.

"You!" She pointed at me again, "You are the great, great, great, great grandchild of Lasater!"

Chapter Fifteen

This could not be! Yet, there it was. In black and white on the well worn page. A complete history of my family descending right down to my grandmother. There a notation had been made that simply said "Traveled West."

"How is this possible?" I asked, dumbfounded by what lay before me. "How is it that my family returned to the very place that my grandmother had abandoned?"

"It is fate, young one." Madam Luna spoke. Her voice had taken on the tone of ages, of mysteries that I could never wish to know nor comprehend. "You are here because you are meant to be here. Nothing more, nothing less. There is no one else of your clan to take your place. It is now your duty." My duty? What am I supposed to do? I want my mommy!

"When Sarah Goode died, she placed a curse upon the girls that falsely accused her. She cursed them to walk the earth forever, begging her forgiveness unless they repent and take responsibility for their actions. All but one did.

This poor child recanted her allegations, yet there were many that believed that she only did so to be accepted back into the fold. That girl was Ann Putnam. Those who knew her best believed that, in her heart, she felt that she was right. Perhaps you should contact her and discover what this is all about." Contact her! How was I to accomplish this feat? Send the girl an engraved invitation? 'Dear Miss Spirit, The honor of your presence is requested at the Hanson home this Tuesday at two o'clock. We wish to discuss your disturbing behavior as of late. Please RSVP as tea and cakes will be served.

Yours sincerely with kindest regards, Bubbles.'

It was not as though she had a door that I could knock upon. Nigel cleared his throat behind me and I turned. I could see the sun sinking low on the horizon through the door and I knew that we had tarried long enough. "Thank you for all your help, Madam Luna." I said, bowing to the elder. "I am afraid that it is time that we go."

"Yes, your family will begin to worry. Go now, and remember what I have said." As though I could forget. I thought of little else for many days following our meeting. I had secluded myself in the upstairs hall, preferring solitude at this time. I did not wish to be petted and coddled as though life were the same as it has always been. I did not remember my mother, let alone my grandmother, yet I recall stories from my kitten hood as though they were yesterday. A soft voice telling me of our family and how important we were in some far off place.

Never did it occur to me that this would one day be of vital importance to me. I was angered beyond thinking when I recalled all that had transpired at that small dwelling in the wood. To have the feeling that one's life was not in one's own control is most maddening indeed.

The worst of it was that I had no idea how to go about contacting this poor spirit and understanding her reasons for her actions. What did she want? If she were truly Sarah Goode returned from the grave to wreak havoc upon the people of modern Salem, what good could we do? Apparently, this woman had been angered at this injustice for quite some time.

I yawned, stretching within the morning sun that streamed through that blasted window. Was Sarah Goode returning and reliving her accusations and subsequent execution? Or was there a darker purpose to her visits? Was she here to torment Christine because of her age and apparent resemblance to one of those foolish girls? This window, with it's wretched pattern, had brought these questions into my mind. The answers escaped my grasp like so much sand through a sieve.

I am not one to be known for thinking well on an empty stomach, and went in search of sustenance. The family was already bustling, going about their daily routines as though nothing were amiss. I found this rather annoying, wishing that I, too, could pretend nothing were out of sorts.

Finding my dish already filled, I set about satisfying my hunger before commencing with the business at hand. So much had occurred as of late, and I was unsure how to go about the next task. Upon completing my meal, I decided to take a stroll out doors. I had hopes the fresh air would clear my head and put things into perspective.

Toby was in the yard, playing with his beloved soccer ball, while Roger taught Christine to ride on Mr. Tibbs. He looked quite content with a rider in his saddle, and I was happy for him.

Indeed, it brought a smile to my lips, as Christine was interacting with her family for the first time in weeks.

I heard humming from an upstairs window and I knew that Julia was most likely converting the fainting room, making final preparations for the new one's arrival. I decided to join her. I had neglected my mistress all too often as of late, and I wanted to remedy that.

As I though, she was sitting on the floor, cross legged, folding tiny clothes and putting them neatly into drawers. I meowed softly, asking permission to intrude upon her private moment. Julia glanced up, motioning for me to join her.

Rubbing against her leg, I forgot for a moment all the troubles and woes that had befallen me and took the simple pleasure and comfort she offered. I began to purr as she stroked my back, reveling in the attention.

"Where have you been?" She asked, as though I would have answered. "So many strange things have happened, don't you think?" I meowed, giving my affirmative response. "Yes, very strange. I'll tell you, Bubbles, I had the strangest dream the other day." My ears perked. Julia was not one given to flights of fancy. If she perceived something as strange, it usually was.

"I was sitting in the parlor reading. I must have dozed off or something. This little one has taken a lot out of me. Well, I heard a creaking noise, like an old rocking chair. It seemed to go on a long time. I saw a strange cat, white, coming toward me. As though it were the most natural thing in the world, he jumped into my lap. I swear, I felt his weight. I petted him for a few moments. Then the creaking stopped. He looked right at me and vanished."

I was shocked. Julia, my Julia, had a sighting.

This was unbelievable. Actually, no, it was a little too believable. It was outrageous. I was more upset than I had been this morning. This had gone on long enough. I needed to seek out someone who knew far more about this place than any one of us did.

I decided to look for Nigel. He knew far more residents than myself. Perhaps he would know who to go to. I quickly found him in Toby's room. He had cornered one of Roscoe's workers and was scolding to make a saint weep.

"I will not stand for this half effort, Mr. Squeaks. This is not our standard, and you are well aware of it. These moldings are to be polished to a shine, do you understand?" "Yes, sire." A high little voice came from the creature. "But, you see, with all of this ghost stuff, I have been distracted." "All the more reason to concentrate on our duties. We would not wish the family to know that anything is out of the ordinary. Why, the young mistress has already had a terrible fright, and the best we can do for her right now is to continue as though nothing is amiss." Nigel had the tone of one who would rub his temples if he could.

"Yes, sir." Mr. Squeaks said, with more than a touch of pout to his voice. "Very well, then. Carry on." Nigel turned, walking out of the room without taking the slightest notice of me. I hurried after as quickly as I could.

"Nigel?" I said, hoping I could get his attention without shouting. He turned and blinked. "Oh, Bubbles. I do apologize. I had not seen you. May I be of some assistance?"

"As a matter of fact, yes. You see, Julia has just had an encounter of her own." I said.

He listened patiently as I recounted what I had just learned. His attention never wavered, and he did not speak until the end. "I presume that this may be the same phantom that we have observed before?"

"I am not sure." I replied. "However, I do think it very well could be. At any rate, this is escalating in number and witnesses. We cannot allow this to continue." I was relieved when he nodded his agreement. "I should say not, Bubbles. What do you propose?"

I did not know what to say. For some reason or another, Nigel and Mrs. Winkle seem to have cast me in the role of leader, and I was weary of the duties. "I was wondering if you perhaps knew of a local historian. Anyone who may be able to tell us a little more of the history of the house and the lives of the people who lived here. That may be a start, at the least."

He pondered for a moment, scratching his chin with his hind foot as he though. After what seemed like a lifetime, he presently said, "I know just the person. Mrs. White."

Chapter Sixteen

Mrs. White was the pet of the head of the Historical Society. The very woman that I had thus far referred to as Blue Dress. The pair of busybodies lived in the center of town in a stately two story house of red brick. The mere fact that we had managed to slip away unnoticed that morning seemed something of a miracle to me.

As we walked along the quaint cobblestone streets, it was quite easy to imagine myself in a very different time. The architecture of the town had changed little from the time of its founding. Had it not been for the modern cars and the town folk strolling about in denim, one could easily step back into the days of old.

We rounded the street corner and came upon the dwelling of Mrs. White and her mistress. I began to ascend the front stairs, but Nigel stopped me with a cough. "This way." He said, and nodded his head in the appropriate direction. Mrs. Winkle and I glanced at one another and followed. We walked along a stone path that wrapped around the back of the house. Sitting on the porch was a plump white long hair Persian.

"Come." Said she. "Sit. I am very glad that you asked to speak with me. The Goode house has always been a topic of particular interest to me." We ascended the steps leading up to the porch. I seated myself in a rather large, cushioned wicker chair. Mrs. Winkle hopped up beside me while Nigel settled on the railing close to Mrs. White.

"Now, my dears. I understand that you are having some problems and need my help." I was slightly taken aback. "How did you know what we needed to speak with you about?" I asked, unsure if this was to be another Madam Luna incident.

"Dearie, this is Salem. A small town. There is very little that goes on that I do not know." She said matter-of-factly.

This revelation has me squirming a bit. I was unsure how to react to the entire township knowing the business of my family. Mrs. White seemed to sense this and said, "Now, don't you worry about that. The humans are not half as observant as we are. They are not aware of all that goes on. Now, to the business at hand."

Nigel cleared his throat. "Mrs. White, we would like to know anything about the Goode family. As we understand it.." Mrs. White interrupted him.

"What you understand is probably all folk lore and fairy tales, Nigel. I do not mean to be rude, but, unfortunately there seems to be a good deal of those that would give you false information. Do not misunderstand. They believe that what they say is true, but the tale of the Goode family has become something like a giant game of telephone, passed down through the ages, the story growing more false with each telling. Lasater was a stray, an unwanted creature that plagued the town fishermen for his meals."

I was growing extremely impatient. While this was all very interesting, this was the history of my lineage, all that mattered was that which would bring this saga to a successful end. I glanced at Nigel, and he rolled his eyes, indicating that our orator had a penchant for the dramatic. I spoke up.

"Mrs. White, I assure you that I do wish to know all of this. What we need at the moment, however, are the basics. In other words, Lasater's involvement in the trials and why on earth my family is being involved in a specter's personal vendetta."

"I understand, darling, I really do. However, I have always found half-information to be only half- useful, don't you agree?" Her honey sweet voice concealed a note of irritation. Damn her, she had a point.

I shook my head. "You must excuse me, Mrs.

White, but I am very tired and given to impatience.

I had not been sleeping well. You understand."

"Indeed." She agreed, nodding her head knowingly. "In fact, just last week, my mistress was in a tizzy over the town's anniversary celebration. She kept me up at all hours of the night, and I have not been right ever since."

Mrs. Winkle broke in at this point. "Poppet, if ya don' min', we do 'ave a good deal to be getting' done. Now, you were sayin' 'bout Lasater?" She prompted our hostess. I marveled at her grace and charm. Was there a situation that she could NOT handle?

"Ah, yes." Mrs. White assented. "Lasater was a thorn in all humans' sides from the day he was born. A rebel, he was. Taking what he wanted and not making apologies for it. In fact, some of the older feline families have stories to tell of him harassing their ancestors.

This is not to say that Lasater was without heart. He was very kind and generous, always sharing the days pilfering with the less fortunate kittens that may have starved otherwise. When a young mother could not nurse all of her kittens, there was Lasater, carrying the tyke to the nearest bowl of cream. When one of the elders of the clan broke his leg, Lasater brought him fish and offered comfort. The felines saw him as their leader. The townsfolk saw him as trouble."

She paused for effect, licking at her spine to prolong the drama. After a fashion, she came back to us, and continued her tale.

"Well, when Samuel's mother was taken in for questioning, Lasater saw the hurt in the lad. True, his mother was not the nurturing sort, but

Samuel loved her nonetheless. He would come to him by night, when he was sitting outside his mother's jail cell, and sleep beside him. When Sarah was carted away to be executed, Lasater stayed by Samuel's side. After Sarah's death, Lasater never left Samuel, and stayed with the boy to offer some measure of comfort. He was the only one the lad would allow near him."

By this time, the hysteria had reached a fevered pitch. When the townspeople saw that Samuel had a feline companion, the very creature said to have been a witch familiar, well, they decided to put a stop to any foolishness that may have entered the boy's head. They stole into the home of his foster parents and took the animal. Lasater complied, not wanting to frighten the child. They tied him up into a small sack, weighted it with rocks and flung it into the sea."

The grim tale had, oddly, little effect on me. The matter of fact way in which she related the events of my ancestor's demise did nothing but confuse me further. Her tale was not finished.

"When Samuel awake the next morning, he went in search of his dear friend. His foster mother suggested that perhaps the creature had merely gone hunting. Hours became days, days became months, and still, no sign.

Eventually, Samuel forgot all about his childhood pet, and built his fortune that provided him the grand house that is now your home. He never forgot his mother, and as I understand it, the tree that was used for the gallows in those dark days is the lumber he used for the archway between the parlor and the sitting room." Of course. The archway! It was all so clear, I felt a fool for not having come to this conclusion before. Of course Sarah Goode was haunting. The scene of her death was now mere decoration. Who would not roll over in their grave?

I glanced at my companions. They shared my surprise, and I am sure they were feeling as foolish as I. Our prior experiences with the archway flooded back to me, and I wondered how I could have missed a detail such as that. The creaking noise that preceded one of the visits should have tipped me off, but the possibility never entered my mind. We needed to get home, fast!

Once we had said our goodbyes and made our promises to come again soon, the three of us began the journey home at top speed. We had already been absent for far too long. The last thing we needed was another incident involving the family. I was unsure what I could do to protect them at this point, however, I wanted to be there in any event.

Following Julia's experience, I had become despondent with regards to ever containing this thing. My resolve to keep the children out of this whole mess was strengthened, however, by Julia's ever swelling belly. She would be ready soon, of that much I was certain. I knew that infant humans were far closer to the feline race than humans ever were for the remainder of their lifespan. I was not about to allow a new member of our family to be frightened in any way.

By the time we had reached the drive leading to the house, I was quite out of breath. Yet something drove me on. I felt an urgency to return as quickly as possible. The burning in my hind legs did not stop me as I ran on as quickly as I could.

We reached the front step. I noted that Toby was sitting at the small table Julia kept there for family board games. So unusual was this sight, I paused.

He was hunched over a piece of paper, his hand moving rapidly across the page. There was a blank look in his deep blue eyes. In fact, the black spots were completely dilated, giving a look of emptiness.

The sight chilled me to my very core. I crept up to him and noticed that he was not even looking at the page. He was staring straight ahead, looking, yet not seeing anything that lay before him. I leapt upon the table and twitched my tail under his nose to bring him about, though it had no effect. Those eyes stayed fixed on some distant object that I could not see. I was beginning to worry, wondering what could have come over him.

Suddenly, Toby gave an ear piercing yelp. He bolted back in his seat and stared down at his leg. I peered over the edge, wondering what could have brought him back to consciousness. There was Nigel, looking very innocent indeed. "Stupid cat." Toby grumbled as he stood and walked away.

"Nigel, really! Was that necessary?" I asked. "Yes, I really do believe it was. Look at the page." I turned the paper with my paw. In a very elegant script, words were neatly written. "You do not understand. You do not understand. I am trapped. Trapped. That witch had trapped me here. Momma, where is my momma? I want to go home.

I want to sleep. Help me, help me HELP ME!"

The message drove chills through me. What is this? I thought to myself. Has Toby been fooling around to scare his sister? As though reading my thoughts, Nigel said, "No. Toby has given ys what we need." I stared, my mind not able to comprehend for the moment. Too much was happening all at once, and I was struggling to keep up. "Yes," he continued, "I do believe he has helped our little friend express herself in ways that we understand." "Surely, you do not mean automatic writing?" I asked. I did not want to believe that awful conclusion was even possible.

"The same. Didn't you see his eyes? He wasn't there. In his place, the person who wrote this message." I gulped at the lump forming at the back of my throat. "You don't mean Toby was possessed, do you?"

"No, no. Automatic writing is not possession in the traditional sense of the word. Rather, it is a temporary condition allowed by the medium through which the spirit acts through him. Not completely harmless, but quite safe given the alternatives."

This was the final straw! The anger welled up within me with such force, I surprised myself, wondering at the thoughts of hatred pulsing through my mind. How dare this little witch involve the family. Something must be done! I waited in the upstairs hall. Alone in my vigil, I had sent Mrs. Winkle and Nigel off to bed. If Madam Luna was to be believed, it was I who could finish this. They would be of little use now.

I stared at the stained glass window, willing the forces of this house to come to me. To end this once and for all. I was determined that this would be the night, this would be the end. Little did I know. The creaking came first. That horrid sound that had preceded so many of my prior encounters with the beyond. Terror filled me for a moment, just a moment, until I recalled why I was there. The anger that filled my heart quickly replaced the fright, leaving in it's wake a wall of red, a shade of crimson I had never before seen. A cold draft surrounded me, chilling me to my very bones. As cold as it was, it did nothing to relieve the anger that filled me. This thing, this mass creeping toward me, had violated the sanctity of my home for the last time. I would square off with this thing, this annoyance and bring my family peace. I could feel it now. A nausea that crept upon me, telling me this thing was on the move. I wanted to run, to hide and be safe. Instead, I held my ground. I am a rather stubborn feline at heart. Somehow, I knew it had reached the base of the stairs. Still I stayed, my back turned towards it, daring it to attack. Logic and reason told me that this thing could not possibly hurt me. Frighten, yes, do physical harm, no. A problem associated with not having a physical body. Panic surged through me, and still I held my ground. I would not be bested by a creature dead for over three hundred years. I was going to see this through, come hell or high litter!

It crept silently up the stairs. The slow pace was the most maddening aspect. Couldn't it do this quickly, and end it all? In point of fact, I became annoyed with the tackless behavior of this creature and almost shouted, "Get on with it!"

I could feel it behind me now, a paw's length away, daring me to turn. I would not give it the satisfaction. You want to deal with me? Then it shall be on my terms! A feeling of centrueis crept over me, of grime and dust. A musty odor filled the hall. I kept my focus on my anger. If I stayed angry, I couldn't lose my nerve. If I stayed angry, I could face it.

I could feel breath parting my fur. It was directly behind me now. In spite of myself, I turned. And came face to face with the eeriest piercing blue eyes I had ever seen!

Chapter Seventeen

"Peace, my son." Said a soft voice. Almost heavenly in tone. "I mean thee no harm. Nor thy kin." I had to stare for a moment, translating the strange speech. "I have come to help thee. Not harm thee, as thou wouldst believe. I am Lasater, thy grandfather, boy. Didst thou not know?"

Was I supposed to answer him? My head was swimming. My throat felt parched, as though I had ran through a desert for a week. I nodded. "I had heard as much from someone. To be quite frank, though, I had not believed it until now."

"Believe, child. Now, I am here to aid thee in thy search. I knew one day thou wouldst return and put an end to her reign of terror. I waited for thee. We must be off."

"Off? To where, might I ask? To meet your friend?"

He snorted in disgust. "That witch is no friend of mine. That little snip of a girl is the reason for my demise. No, her's is not the presence we must seek tonight. Tonight is for knowledge, to better prepare thee for they task. Come, we must not linger."

A white light blinded me for a moment, and I felt as though I were falling. Not fast and frightening, but slow and gently. It was almost like floating, truth be told. I blinked and yet, saw nothing. Before I know what was happening, I felt solid ground beneath my feet.

Opening my eyes, I looked about me. A large, luminous figure crouched, as though waiting for the kill. I started, until my vision cleared. There was a large, deformed oak tree. Behind us, I heard a cacophony of voices. I turned around, glancing at Lasater as I did so, but he kept his gaze straight ahead.

The light of torches crept up the side of the hill, throwing ugly shadows of monsters into the fading light.

Chapter Eighteen

Cries of "Witch!" and "Sorceress" filled the air.

Three hooded figures were being led, or rather, dragged, up the hill towards the tree. Some were singing mournful hymns in that dreadful monotone that the puritans seem to take for dutiful joy. One was carting three lengths of rope. The sight of this sent a dreadful shiver down my spine, as though a length of it were reserved for me.

One of the hooded three was fighting back.

Twisting and undulating in a vain attempt to break free from her captors. Wet marks stained the hood of the second, obviously where eyes were, and I knew that this one had resigned herself to her fate. My heart went out to her. I wished that I could stop this madness, yet I knew there was nothing I could do.

I rounded Lasater, staring into his eyes and I knew. I knew that he had brought me to this time. A time when terror and fear gave way to anger and insanity in a way the world had not seen before or since that dark, dreadful time. I plead with my eyes, silently asking, why? Why have you brought me here? His blank stare was my only answer.

The mob drew near and I could smell the sweat of these humans, these creatures of evil. They passed through us as though we were no more than a mist hovering over the ground. It was an eerie feeling, to say the least. They gathered round the tree and I knew what was coming. The hooded figured were violently shoved to the front, and fell to their knees.

One dark figure moved forward. Lighted by the torches, it only added to the ominous, grim air that already permeated his very being. I shuttered at the mere sight of him. He removed his hat. Opening the Bible that had been tucked neatly under his arm, he looked up, his gaze taking in the entire congregation. Piercing green eyes peered out from beneath thick, bushy brows, boring into their souls as though he could read every impure thought they had ever had.

"Evil walk among us." His voice boomed as he raised his arms high into the air. This silenced the crowd instantly. "These cold-hearted wenches thought to put us under their spell and enslave us in their world of wickedness. They have been tried and found guilty of the crime of witchcraft! They have danced, naked, under the full moon with their hooved master. They have endangered our children. They have attacked us! Goody Hoar, Goody Esty and Goody Goode, thou art hereby condemned to hang from the neck until thou art dead. Dost thee understand?"

The hoods were removed. I recognized Sarah at once, having studied her portrait in the window for uncountable hours. She slowly raised her head, leveling her stare at the dark man before her. "I understand, Reverend Parris. I understand that thine own household is the very hearth that brought this plague to Salem. Dost thou deny that thine own servant, Tituba, taught thy charges the dark art of divination? I spit on thee, Reverend, and I promise to see thee in hell!"

Her mad cackle filled the night. The mob heaved a collective gasp, staring at the Reverend, not wanting to believe the revelation before them.

"Silence, mad witch!" he roared, kicking her squarely in the chin. "Thou shalt not confuse these weak being with thine dark craft. You will hang, and we and God almighty shall be glad of it!"

He gestured and two men brought forth the ropes. Tossing and looping them around a low, thick branch, they pulled tight. Securing the slack around the base of the tree, their grim work was complete. Three low stools were brought forth and placed directly beneath the nooses. The condemned were shoved forward once more. Dragged to their feet, they were ultimately placed upon the stools. With the ropes secured around their necks, the Reverend opened his Bible yet again.

"The Lord is my shepherd, I shall not want, he maketh me to lie in green pasture..." The congregation bowed their heads and murmured along with the prayer. I bowed my head too, not to their prayer, but a silent one of my own. I prayed for the madness to stop, for these idiots to come to their senses, for this to end any way but how I knew it would.

"Sinners!" The roar came with such force, I was nearly bowled over. "Repent now, and thy souls shall be seated by our Lord in heaven. Repent not, and thou shalt burn for a thousand years in the heated embrace of thine own dark lord. How say thee?"

Two repented immediately, streams of tears tracing rivers through the grime on their faces. Sarah looked up defiantly. "I have not sinned any more than this entire congregation. The Lord will deal with me fairly and justly. It is thine daughters who must repent. I curse thee, bringers of sin and madness. I curse thee to walk this earth for a thousand years shouldst thou not repent of thine sins. Beg the forgiveness of thy congregation and of me, and thou shalt be spared. Beg it not, and thou shalt never know peace."

The last word was choked out as three large men simultaneously kicked out the stools from beneath them. I heard a sickening crack as their necks broke, but Sarah's feet kicked for several moments. Her eyes bulging from the sockets and her tongue lolling out of her mouth as she gasped her final breath.

Chapter Nineteen

I blinked. Familiar smells surrounded me. I was home! Turning wildly, I sought out Lasater, yet he was nowhere to be found. I was left alone with the memories of the atrocities that I had just witnessed. The image of Sarah Goode breathing her last haunted me. I was left shaken by the scenes that had flashed before me. It had all seemed so real, and yet was no more palpable than a dream.

I needed to find Nigel and Mrs. Winkle. I needed to tell them of what had just happened. I ran down the stairs at a speed I had not not attained since youth. The urgency that drove me coursed through my blood like so much catnip. I had just seen death and stood in the presence of true evil. I had returned to tell of my adventure.

They were in the study. "I have looked everywhere for Bubbles, Mrs. Winkle. Every stone has been turned." Said Nigel. Was it my imagination, or was there actually concern in his eyes?

"I know, ducky. I turned this place upside down, I did. With no sign."

"Here I am." I shouted, breathless. "I need to..."

But my breath caught and I fell upon the floor, limp. "Dearie!" Shouted Mrs. Winkle as she rushed to my side. "I say," Nigel piped in, "You look like death warmed over. Bubbles, what has happened? We have been searching for you for hours."

The words stuck in my throat. I was gasping for air, trying to fill my lungs. I looked at them, pleasing for help. Mrs. Winkle was gently stroking my spine in a vain attempt to calm me. Nigel was looking around helplessly, unaware of how to aid me.

Memories and images swirled in my mind. I could recall my mother. Her scent, her purr. I saw myself bathed by her. I closed my eyes, wishing to return to her, to a much simpler time when my only worry was my next meal and my next nap. I wanted to go home.

"Thou art home, child." A familiar voice interrupted my pleasant dreams. "Thou art home and well." My eyes opened to see Lasater standing before me. I must have blacked out. "Thou art here to end this misery and bring peace to the Goode house after three hundred years."

Nigel and Mrs. Winkle were nowhere to be found. They must have bolted out of fright and left me to deal with the consequences. "What, dear grandfather, is your damage?" I asked sweetly as I attempted to stand and found the effort useless. He cocked his head to one side, puzzled by the teenage expression I had heard so often from Christine. "I do not understand. Thou dost have a strange manner of speaking."

"No more strange than yours, old man." I mumbled under my breath. "What I am inquiring is, why on earth did you take me there? What was the point of all that? Was it really necessary to frighten the daylights out of me?" "I apologize." He said, bowing low. "I believed it was necessary for thou to understand. We have another long journey before us. We must leave at once."

"Good 'eavens!" Mrs. Winkle exclaimed from the doorway. "Nigel! Nigel, come quick, dearie!"

Both rushed into the room. "What is all this?" Nigel asked, peering at the strange feline with malice. His whiskers twitched as he attempted to sniff Lasater's scent, the feline equivalent of an identification card. Lasater held up a paw.

"Tis useless, young one. I have no scent. Tis a result of being dead."

Nigel recoiled as though struck, twitching his whiskers back and forth. "No matter. I was merely attempting to recognize your presence. At any rate." He cleared his throat. "Ah." Lasater nodded his head in understanding. "I believe that we must take thine companions with us, grandchild. It shall be more efficient."

I shook my head violently. "No!" I would not allow them to be brought into this. Bad enough that I had been dragged into this, my family. Not my friends. Never. "Child, tis the only way. They must understand, as thou does, exactly the happenings of that time. To accomplish this, they must come with us."

"Well, I certainly am not goin' to sit 'round 'ere on me keester while you two go galavantin'! Now, Bubbles, no. Who says you get to go and 'ave all the fun?" Mrs. Winkle gave me a look that said I had best do as I was told. I was not about to argue.

"Bubbles," Nigel said, "I must tell you that the family has gone. Julia is about to have the baby, and I do believe that tonight is the time to sort this out. We can't let that child come into a situation like this."

My heart ceased. Julia! And I was not there for her. "I hate to say you're right, Nigel. So, I won't. Alright, Lasater, let's go."

A howling wind raged about us. I could see nothing. An inky blackness surrounded us, and there we were. As the mist cleared, I saw we were in a small room, a candle giving the only light. A small boy was playing in a corner, his wooden figures moving back and forth in his private game. Lasater was looking on with sadness in his eyes, and I knew this boy was Samuel.

We watched for a few more moments, Nigel and Mrs. Winkle taking in the scene around them. "Samuel, supper is on the table." A voice called out. He put his things away neatly, so unlike other little boys who would have merely pushed them farther into the corner. "Yes, ma'am. I am coming." He called back. Samuel stood and, after a final check to make sure all was well, he left the room.

"How I miss that child." Lasater said. The heartache in his voice tugged at my very soul. "I can to him after Sarah's death. It was too much for him to bear alone." Lasater turned and strode quickly out of the room. We followed in close pursuit, not wanting to lose sight of him. We walked down a narrow, dark hallway and descended an equally narrow set of stairs.

We found Lasater in the keeping room where Samuel and two adult humans were sitting to their evening meal. I could detect the enticing aroma of a beef stew with carrots and fresh peas, homemade biscuits and a fresh peach cobbler that was baking upon the hearth. I had never smelled food that had never been touched by preservatives or man-made seasonings and the scent was intoxicating. I shook my head, reminding myself that we were here for information, not dinner.

The mood surrounding the table was solemn. Something told me that this was not the usual routine and the silence was unnerving. Samuel squirmed in his seat, the obvious result of a child kept out of the loop. The man sat hunched over his plate, shoveling his meal into his mouth, not tasting it. What a waste. The woman was picking at her food, pushing the meal around her plate to conceal how little she had eaten.

"Pa?" Samuel piped up meekly, worried that he may be chastised. "Yes, Samuel?"

"How was the grazing in the east field today?" The child was attempting to make conversation to lighten the mood that had descended upon his home. The man looked up at the woman, who shrugged her shoulders in response.

"T'was good. The cattle will be nice and fat before winter. We can thank the good Lord for that."

Again, an uneasy silence fell upon the table and the boy heaved a sigh of frustration. The woman looked at her husband and then spoke. "Samuel? The Turner's cat has just birthed a litter of kittens. Wouldst thou like to come with me tomorrow and choose one?" The child's eyes lit up for a moment, but darkened again when the motive became clear to him. "Why? We have Lasater. He is a fine cat, and a good mouser. We haven't had any mice in the pantry since he came to us." The adults glanced at each other, worried that they might have been discovered.

"Tis true, Lasater is a fine cat. Yet, he is old, son, and we were wanting him to teach a younger cat than himself before the Lord calls him home."

The child looked around frantically. "Thou dost not mean he is sick, do ye? I was playing with him today and he looked well." The worry expressed told of a deep love for his friend. Lasater strode to the child's side and gazed upward into his face. I could see that he loved the lad, and my heart ached for my own family.

"No, son. Thy pet is safe. I was only thinking no creature lives forever, and thou may like another friend to play with and another cat around the house." The man sat upright in his chair, becoming more confident in his lie. Samuel looked from the woman to the man. His posture softened a bit and he breathed a sigh of relief. "Oh, well. If tis only that, I would like to go with mama and choose a friend for Lasater." As though that closed the subject, the boy began to shovel food into his mouth in a manner I had often seen in Toby.

The remainder of the meal passed in silence, though not as thick with apprehension as before.

Samuel, satisfied that his friend was safe and healthy, completed his supper and proceeded to consume two helpings of his peach cobbler with fresh cream. After the dishes were washed and dried, and the boy retreated to his room to prepare for bed.

As he folded his clothing and placed them neatly on a chair for the next day, he climbed into bed. From the door, we heard a meow. Turning, I was startled to see a living Lasater come in. Samuel patted a spot next to him on the bed and the feline gracefully floated to his appointed position. After blowing out the candle, the boy lay down and began to stroke Lasater.

"We are going to get thou a friend tomorrow, Lasater. Would you like a friend?" Samuel asked in the dark. The living Lasater purred his pleasure, snuggling in closer. Our Lasater turned to me then.

"I knew. I knew what was about to happen. I did not want to run, or worry the child in any way. I knew that with all the madness, if the townsfolk could not find me, they would take their wrath out on him. So, I waited."

Chapter Twenty

In moments, we were in the keeping room again. The man and woman were speaking in hushed tones, and I could tell that something was wrong.

"The child will be heartbroken." Said the wife, shaking her head as she scrubbed the bare wooden table with a rag. "I know, Meredith. I know. But dost thou not agree that this is for the best? With his mother gone, that cat has become his world. He needs to become a part of the world again. The human world. He needs playfellows of his own age, and race."

"This madness is infecting everyone, and I do not wish it to come into mine own house." Said the woman. She was scrubbing so hard, her knuckles turned white. "This madness, as you call it, is not simply going to stop. The town is frightened, and they will unleash their fury on us if we do not comply. I would rather sacrifice that cat than sacrifice our son."

I was puzzled at first. Surely, the townsfolk would not try and execute a mere child in their misguided state. Surely, logic and reason would prevent them from that. Lasater turned to me and shook his head. In that single, simple gesture, I understood what was in his thoughts. Samuel was the son of a convicted and executed witch. This alone threatened to condemn him. Should these good people refuse to hand over the feline for their judgment, they would think that he were some sort of familiar to the boy and prosecute not just the child, but the household as well.

Never, in all my considerable days, had I imagined that such a thing were possible. Never could I have dreamed that such thought and logic could pervade the human mind and be not only acceptable, but endorsed. As I pondered over this, I could see torch lights approaching. I held my breath, for I knew what was to follow.

Three loud bangs shook the front door of the rather sturdy home. The man rose from the table to answer it. "For the love of God, man, dost thou not know the child is sleeping?" He said into the darkness. "I care not, Dostie. Give us the cat." The man shrugged his shoulders in a gesture of defeat. "I will give thou the cat. Wait here a moment." He whispered.

The woman retreated up the stairs, returning a moment later with Lasater in her arms. "Thou wilst not harm him much?" She asked. "It will be quick?"

"Ay, a swift death for a quick witch. Do not worry, Goody Dostie. The child need never know that his mother's evil spirit is gone from this earth forever. I pray only for his sake that her malice did not penetrate his soul."

No sound was made as Lasater was passed from the woman's arms into a small canvas sack. The men tipped their hats and began to leave. The woman went to her husband and melted into his arms as she sobbed.

We followed the group to the edge of the water where more individuals awaited their arrival. No Bible reading for Lasater. No hymns nor word of the Lord spoken. Just an unceremonious fastening of stones to the sack to weight it down and a toss into the icy depths. The crowd watched as the sack disappeared into the blackness and then simply trundled home as though it were a nightly ritual.

"It did not hurt. It was like going to sleep. No pain, no resistance. Just sleep and dreams." Lasater spoke as if to himself, lost deep in his memories of the past and the pain of having to leave his dear friend. "I had to leave. To protect him. They would have hounded him as the devil's own minions until he confessed to a crime he did not commit. Such was their hate and malice, they would have sacrificed a child to feed their vengeance."

I stepped forward, searching his face. I understood, all too well, the sacrifices one would make for the safety of the ones they love. No word was spoken for none was needed.

"I shall take thee back. Enough of these memories of life and death long past."

As quickly as we were there, we had returned. The house seemed deathly quiet, the family gone and we four alone. The events I had just witnessed haunted my thoughts. Unable to shake them and unwilling to understand the motives behind them. I had never felt true evil before, and yet, on that hill, standing before the icy waves of the Atlantic Ocean, I knew that I had stood in the presence of evil and all it represented.

I felt chilled to the bone. I was unsure as to whether that was a result of the journey or what I had just witnessed. I was shaking all over and felt sick to my very stomach. I decided to sit and clear my head before speaking with anyone. Nigel and Mrs. Winkle were fervently discussing all that had transpired with Lasater, yet I could not hear a word. My sense of hearing had left me. I saw only their lips moving, not a mumble passing through the blanket of silence that enveloped my world.

I do not know what happened first, the creaking noise, or the sickening glow of the archway before me. The pale blue glow enshrouded it, pulsating as though a heart were attached to it. The creaking was growing in intensity. I looked around me, attempting to determine whether all heard it, or it was just myself having this vision. I saw no signs of shared experience, nor could I hear what was being said. The awful creaking would not stop and reverberated through my skull.

I wanted to scream, and yet, my vocal cords seemed to have been rendered useless. Unable to alert my companions, I shut my eyes in the misguided notion that this action would make it go away. Pain coursed through my brain, and I felt that I would split in two.

My eyes snapped open as though I had been pinched. Lasater, Nigel and Mrs. Winkle were staring at me expectantly. "Well, love, what do ya think?" Shaking my head, I responded. "Think about what, pre-tell?" I asked. I was confused about what had just happened and why. "About what, indeed!" Mrs. Winkle chortled. "Our plan. We got to do something. What with the family away and all. 'tis our duty."

"Oh, yes. Fine idea. Splendid, simply splendid." I said, a rather weak attempt to conceal my surprise. Little did I know what these three had been up to during the length of my malady. "That settles it then." Said Nigel as he proceeded to exit the parlor. We followed. I wondered where we were going and if it was to be during the present time frame or otherwise. These questions I kept to myself, trudging behind the others while I attempted vainly to sort out our destination.

We walked for what seemed like hours. The crickets chirped in the high grass as the fire flies flicked along the hills. I took the opportunity to think through the course my life had taken in the last few months. Outwardly, little had changed. Yet, beneath the surface lay waves of turmoil that was sweeping the peace of our lives out to sea.

As I all too soon discovered, our destination was an open field far from the safety of our home.

Faded wooden crosses mingled with sleek marble stones in their silent vigil over those who had gone before us. I felt a chill run the length of my body. We stopped in front of a large marble sculpture of an angel in repose, her eyes cast downwards as her glittering wings enveloped the length of her body. "Here lieth Sarah Goode. Martyr and Mother, gone to Peace and Understanding Above."

"I don't understand. Why are we here of all places?" I asked, convinced that we were upon dangerous ground indeed.

"Hast thou not been attentive? Dost thou not know what all that you have learned and been shown means? Sarah Goode is not the specter that torments thee, child. 'tis Ann Putnam thee must be worried over!"

Chapter Twenty-One

"Ann Putnam? What in the name of Bast are you talking about? It is Sarah Goode in the stained glass window. It is Sarah Goode that was Samuel's mother. It was Sarah Goode that was executed for false crimes. What does Ann Putnam have to do with all of this?"

"I believe I can answer thine questions." A melodic voice came from behind the gravestone. A voice so sweet, one could picture the owner without ever having seen her and have an accurate picture in one's mind. Rounding the corner of the statue, the black folds of her dress made no sound, came one who could only be Ann Putnam herself!

The white bonnet framed her delicate features and I could scarcely believe that this child was responsible, even partly, for one of the darkest periods in human history. She seated herself at the base of the stone, her dress flowering around her knees in a most becoming fashion. Instinctively, we moved into the folds of the fabric, intent upon hearing her story.

"I didn't mean it. At least, not at first. It was all in fun. Our playing at finding out who our husband would be. In those days, that was the focus of our world. Whom was courting whom, whom was with child, and we could not wait to join those ranks.

When we were discovered, it would have destroyed the community if their own daughters were involved in witchcraft, so we claimed to have been bewitched.

Tituba was our victim. After all, she was from Barbados, and a negress. Who simpler to blame our toyings on than her? It was never supposed to have gone so far. I am still certain to this day that had it not been for my mother, many lives could have been spared. Unfortunately, mother was an invalid, stricken by an illness so frightening and mysterious, I still get shivers recalling her bouts with it. The long nights of crippling fevers, the pain and exhaustion she suffered. She allowed it to destroy her. It turned her bitter towards the world and all the people in it.

Seeing her opportunity when we had Tituba so easily convicted, she convinced me that I truly had the power to divine those that were in league with the dark one. With her help, of course. She would suggest those that she had perceived had wronged her and I was to accuse them before the council.

The other girls followed along, I believe to simply avoid the discovery of our ruse.

It was all so terrible. We would pass by our victims and then throw ourselves to the ground in convulsions. We would scream and pull at our hair, drawing blood from our faces with our nails and screeching that their specter was tormenting us.

The town fathers would promptly arrest them and try them before the high council in the meeting house. Sarah Goode, despite her outward appearance of a tramp, remained dignified throughout her trial."

At this junction in her story, Ann sighed. No doubt remembering those dark days when she held the lives of her fellow townsfolk in her hands. It was a tempting thought to a young girl, I suppose. One could easily abuse such power.

"To say that I was torn in two would be an understatement. After Goody Hoar, Goody Esty and Goody Goode were executed, I realized that this was no mere game. The townsfolk took this quite seriously and were even willing to kill to protect our way of life. The situation was so out of control that we were even lent to a neighboring town to divine witches there. I was a Puritan. I was raised to do as my parents told me. To have my mother encouraging and even instructing me as to whom to accuse next, I was confused.

Goody Goode was right. I never truly repented in my heart for all the deaths I caused. In the end, over twenty souls of Salem were condemned and executed at our encouragement. A part of me recoiled at the horror of it all. Another part of me felt righteous, good and pure for having put the dark minions down."

Ann paused, silent tears streaming down her face. I pitied her. Wanting to offer some measure of comfort, I crawled into her lap. The poor innocent child was being forced to suffer, all as a result of her duty to her mother. She gently stroked my spine and I purred with pleasure. She continued.

"I have had over three hundred years to repent what I have done. Every day of it, I have. I have come here, to the final resting place of Sarah Goode, praying with all the strength of my soul, hoping, wishing that I could go home. Yet I am still here. I do not understand."

Lasater approached. "Child. I, myself, do not understand why thee is still here. However, thou canst pester the living. Thou did so in life, and thou is still doing it in death. We know of what you have done with the children of Bubbles' family. Why, thou hast even involved the mother. Why? What was thou hoping to accomplish by touching Julia as thou did? Do you not know the danger a specter could put a woman with child by behaving so?"

I bristled at this. The poor child was simply missing her mother. She was scared and alone. She wanted nothing more than to be at peace, and here Lasater was chiding her. I do not know what it was, but suddenly, I could forgive her all the things she had put my family through. Perhaps it was her eyes. Those great big doe eyes looking so innocent and pure. I stared into them now, searching for any window into this girl's true heart. Searching for the answers that would finally allow her to leave this place, the very site of her fall from grace. What I found there left me cold.

Chapter Twenty-Two

I spoke up then, needing a moment with my companions to sort this out. "Ann, if you will excuse us for a moment. I need to speak with my fellows." Gesturing, I pulled them aside for a conference.

We gathered in the grass, not very far off, yet far enough for her not to hear. "Lasater, I think I know why she is still here. I also think I understand why she is doing the things she is doing to the family." The surprise on their collective faces! Let's just say that I wish I had a camera to capture that moment!

"Well, don' be 'oldin' out on us, ducky!" Huffed Mrs. Winkle. "Might you be able to tell us of your revelation, Bubbles. We may finally be done with this sordid business once and for all!" This was Nigel and as I looked at him, I could tell he was getting rather impatient.

"Look, I am asking you for your patience right now. I am not fully comprehending this all myself. I don't even know where to begin or how to say this. I think that Ann still believes in her heart that she was right all along."

This time, their composure did not fail. I waited, wishing one of them would say something so as not to make me feel like a fool. I could hear Ann, mumbling away in her doleful prayer, attempting to soothe her soul. At last, it was Mrs. Winkle who spoke.

"I do think it would be best if we showed the child how she did wrong. Think about it, Bubbles. Do the children always know why they are in trouble when Julia does chide 'em?" Confound it all, the feline made sense! Often, Julia had to walk the children, figuratively speaking, through their offense before they fully comprehended why it was they were on restriction.

"Yes. Do you recall when Christine was not allowed to go to the picture show with her friends?" Chimed in Nigel. "She was far more upset about her punishment than she was about her infraction." I recalled this. Christine had tormented the whole of the house, railing against the injustice and many a door had felt the effect of her wrath.

"Lasater." I said, having a fit of inspiration. "Do you know anything of restorative justice?" I had a plan in mind to save this girl's soul. "What dost thou mean, grandchild?"

"Well, I recall Julia speaking of the principles of this philosophy around the dinner table one evening. I was underneath, looking for the odd, wayward morsel, and I was forced to listen to the conversation. The essence of the principle is showing the offender the effects of their actions, not just in the sense that they are being punished, but also, the negative effects of their actions on the community as a whole."

It took a moment for him to absorb my meaning. When he did, a light of realization shone in his eyes. "Ah. I see thy point. Thou wants to show her the full harm she has caused. It makes perfect sense. How wouldst thou have me accomplish this task?"

"Well, if you can take us back, isn't it possible to take her? The physical effects of it should not bother her at all, and it might show her a few things in the process."

"It should be easier, poppet." Added Mrs. Winkle. "After all, it's not like we 'ave much of a choice. Must be now or never." It still tickled me, hearing Mrs. Winkle address Lasater like he was some kitten, rather than being an elder. "I do suppose it is the best plan we have got. The child must repent completely before she is allowed to go on. I do not believe that she is capable of understanding everything that she has caused without seeing it firsthand." I could always count on Nigel to state the blatantly obvious in a manner that could convince a willow tree. "Very well." Said Lasater. "I shall need thy help. I am not accustomed to young girls, having been the beloved pet of the kindest boy ever known. Wouldst thou all agree to aid me?" He implored. Nodding our ascension, we four rose and made our way back to Ann and the somber marble angel.

"Ann." I said, hypnotized by those mesmerizing eyes she turned upon me. "We will help you. You must come with us." We had interrupted her mid-prayer. Her hands clasped before her, so tightly her already pale knuckles gleamed white in the moonlight. In her long black gown and white bonnet, she was the picture of puritanical devotion. Her face showed the expression of hope that I know she felt within her heart. For a moment, I again wondered how this simple child could have done the despicable things she had.

"Thou must come with us, child. We are here to help thee." Said Lasater. For a moment, Ann's face registered complete horror. "I know thee."

Said she, terrified beyond her wits. "Was thou not Sarah Goode, come from the grave to watch over her eldest son?" Lasater shook his head. "No, child. Tis true enough, I was companion to that lonely child in his darkest hour, but no soul other than mine own had ever occupied my mortal coil. T'was I that the townsfolk executed without so much as a trial. However, that is not of consequence now. This moment is for understanding. This moment, we are more concerned with righting thine wrongs and making amends with thy victims."

"I do not understand." Ann implored. "I did as I was told. The good book says to honor thy father and mother. That is the only crime I was ever guilty of." This statement alone told me what we were working with. I knew now more than ever, this child needed to understand and see reason before she could properly make amends and repent her sins that would release her soul.

"Ann, this is the very point we are trying to make." Said I, "We are going to help you. We know what is binding you to this place, but you must trust us. We will not steer you wrong."

Again, that sickening feeling of being pulled. The flash of light almost blinded me, and once more, we were on Gallows Hill. The three figures moved in the darkness, one writhing under the grasp of her captors. I was not paying attention to the scene. I had already borne witness. Instead, I opted to watch Ann's face throughout. I wanted to see her expression. I wanted to see the dawn of comprehension on her face. This was the pain she had wrought. Again, the voice of the preacher boomed through the cool night air, the surf pounding in the background only served to heighten the sensation of doom. Again, Sarah Goode proclaimed her innocence. Again, we heard the deafening cry of her shrill voice. Cursing the congregation that had brought about her demise.

"It is thine daughters who must repent. I curse thee, bringers of sin and madness. I curse thee to walk this earth for a thousand years shouldst thou not repent of thine sins. Beg the forgiveness of thy congregation and of me, and thou shalt be spared. Beg it not, and thou shalt never know peace."

A small glimmer of revelation lit up this young girl's eyes, but not nearly enough to know our job was done. I knew, then, that she would have to see the complete story before she would feel the full weight of all that had come to pass in those dark days. Looking at Lasater, I conveyed this message with my eyes. Humans think we felines are capable of telepathy, however, I was never able to actually accomplish this until now. I saw that he understood my thoughts, and he nodded his comprehension. This next journey would be a doozy.

The meeting house was packed to bursting. It seemed all of Salem was there to witness the atrocity. To be honest, I would have attended as well. Life in 1692 was rather dull and the days were filled with chores, chores and sleep. Meals were somber times, more to nourish the body for chores than to enjoy the food offered. As such, any occasion to be away from the hearth and among the people was a welcome treat.

At the front of the church were two long tables.

Behind these sat several men, all wearing knee breaches and white stockings. Their powdered wigs cast a small halo of dust about each of their heads and I could smell it's musty odor. In fact, I sneezed frequently from the microscopic onslaught. In a small area to the right sat several young girls. I judged them to be between 11 and 19. I could clearly make out Ann among their numbers, and I knew these were the accusers of Salem.

Suddenly, the man in the middle, the only one to be wearing a black robe, boomed in a very deep voice. "Bring forth the accused!" A small door opened on the left back wall and in came an elderly gentleman, heavily shackled, head hung in shame or exhaustion. I could not tell which. The moment he was brought into the room, the young women began to have fits. They screeched and writhed, some throwing themselves upon the floor. Some were pulling on their hair so hard, I could hear the follicles being ripped from the skin. Others were scratching themselves. And there was Ann. Our sweet, innocent, doe-eyed Ann, right in the thick of it, and acting a fool like all the rest.

Now, my logical self was sitting there pondering, throughout this fracas of stupidity, that surely, the adults would see this for what it was. That they would see it was merely children pretending and would not believe a word of it. In my hear of hearts, I knew this would not happen. Yet, I could not helop but hope that logic and reason would win the day.

The center man spoke again, raising his pitch so

as to be heard over the mob of estrogen fueled foolishness, "Giles Corey. Dost thou deny that thou is a wizard?" I looked to the shackled old man. He raised his graying head, and said nothing.

"Corey, this is your last chance to save yourself. Confess and repent and thou shalt be given a quick and painless death! Repent not, and thou shalt be hanged." I must admit here, this did not sound like much motivation to me. Die or die. Those are fantastic choices. Obviously not the height of criminal inquisition in this country. Still, Giles said nothing. No emotion, no expression marred his peaceful face. Still, the group of girls continued with their silliness. Many were screaming that the specter of Giles Corey was afflicting them, pinching them, pulling their hair. This was utter nonsense. First, the obvious. Humans have no invisible twin of themselves. Thus, if Corey were afflicting them, the whole of the gathering would have seen it. Second, if you were accused of witchcraft, and were hoping to save your neck, would you afflict the girls in the midst of your own trial? Again, logic and reason. These were two elements that were sadly missing during the year 1692 in Salem.

I heard a sharp intake of breathe and looked up at Ann. "Ay, we were foolish girls. I still cannot believe that I would behave like this. How could anyone not see that we were only pretending?" This statement gave me hope. "Tis true enough, their specters never did plague us. However, there was still much more that the council could have used to convict these vile being of their crimes." And, the glimmer of hope was gone.

Again, Lasater nodded and we were pulled from that place. We found ourselves in a field. The sun dried grass dug into my tender paws, and I could hear the crunch of it as we walked. A disgusting odor crept up my nostrils and I realized I was smelling human rot.

We walked to a small grouping of men, clustered around something in the earth. I assumed it was a grave, but the reality was much more terrifying. As we approached, I could hear grunts and groans. I soon realized these sounds were the sound of a man doing his best to draw breathe. Looking down, between their legs, I saw a man I recognized as Giles Corey. He was under a pile of large stone and beneath that heap, I could see planks of wood. The magistrate, the man in the black robe from the meeting house, was standing over him.

"Dost thou confess, Giles Corey?" He boomed again. Again, I could hear the grunts of the man doing his all to fill his lungs. This went on for a few minutes until we could hear, faintly, Giles Corey say, "More Wieght!" This shocked and awed me. The guts, the glory, the sheer conviction.

He was refusing to say one way or the other as to his guilt. The confusion must have registered on my face, for Lasater spoke up then.

"Twas the law in Salem. Unless thou obtained a confession from the accused, their property would not go to the crown upon their execution. The magistrate wanted Corey's estate. He was a man of means, and they wanted his things. His wife was also accused, and executed by hanging. Neither of them ever confessed and upon their deaths, all their property went to their sons-in-law." Ah, now it made perfect sense. The township would profit from the deaths of some of the better off citizens if they confessed to their crimes. No wonder they were so ready to believe the falsehoods of the prepubescent fools!

"Not true!" Railed Ann. It was the first time she spoke since the meeting house. "That is not true. They did not want their property. They wanted to make the village safe for us. We could not have the minions of Satan running through out town, controlling our destinies. It was good and right what they did!" With this last word, we heard a sound that I shall never forget in all of my nine lives. The death rattle of Giles Corey. Our next stop was at a modest home built of dark wooden planks. Ann rushed to the front door and began running her hand over the smooth wood. "Home. I am home, at long last." And with that, she passed straight through the door. We had to scurry quickly after her. The moment we entered the house, we could see her dark skirts disappearing up the stairs and we quickly gave chase. No words were needed to know what could happen here and we wanted to be there in case Ann could not handle this. I had no idea what Lasater meant bringing her here like this. What I did know was that this could be a potentially volatile situation.

We entered a small bedroom, modestly appointed with a small bed, obviously filled with straw from the odor it gave off. A very small and frail woman lay nestled among many pillows, garbed in a simple nightgown with a high collar and long sleeves cinched at the wrist.

Her dark auburn hair lacked the sheen that you knew it once possessed in her youth and wayward strands stuck to her sweat soaked brow. She resembled Ann greatly, and it was quite clear that she had been a strikingly beautiful woman once. Her chest rattled with a deep cough that even I could feel within me, and I knew the poor woman was suffering.

"Mother, I am here. I have come home at last. This must be heaven. I am once again by your side." Ann rushed forward to perch on the bed, yet, her form did not sink into the soft bedding. She merely floated on the top. The elder Ann stared right through her and turned her head. I could hear her muttering to herself. "Where is that girl?" As Lasater stepped forward, I could see the pain in the young girl's face. "Mother, I am right here. Dost thou not see me?"

"She cannot see you child. She is but a shadow of things that are long past. Thou is home, but not at rest. I have brought you here for understanding, not for comfort or peace."

Lasater lit upon the bed. "Thou must understand the truth of all the havoc thou hast wrought. Thou must know the reality of thine actions." At this, the poor girl crumpled, her head in her hands, her body wracked with sobs that could produce no tears.

Another fitful cough burst forth from the frail woman. So violent was it, I was surprised that she did not split in two from the sheer force of it. Again, she mumbled to herself. "There are more. There are many more the child must put down.

How couldst he do this? I, who was the most becoming girl in the village. I, whom could have been the wife of the governor himself. And I chose him. I put my heart and my life in his hands, and he did betray me. They shall pay. They shall all pay."

It was here that Lasater spoke again. "You see, Mr. Putnam had wed Ann with the taste of her dowry in his mouth. Once that was squandered, he had to resort to a trade. Never one to work for his keep, Mr. Putnam decided to politic instead. He was on the council to convict. As such, he stood to gain from those who confessed. He used this to sway Mrs. Putnam to do his bidding. He promised her a better life with the money he received, but in the end, he squandered that too."

The picture was becoming far more clear now. Ann's father had broken the commandment forbidding greed, and his wife was paying the price. It was no wonder the woman was bitter, no wonder she wanted to wreak her vengeance on those that had wronged her. I did not agree with it, but done is done and nothing could be revoked. "I do not understand." This was not the first time Ann had uttered these words. "Mother would sometimes come to the trials and she was often afflicted too. She accused as well as I. She was a righteous woman. She would not have falsely accused anyone."

Lasater climbed into Ann's lap and gazed into her eyes. "Tis not unusual for a child to believe only the best of her parents. Thou were but a babe of twelve summers at the time, yes? Thou couldst not have seen or understood the malice and fear that festers within the human heart. When one has grown and toils the land for survival, one becomes bitter. Especially when one dost live in a place such as Salem, where the rich are gluttonous and the poor must eat potatoes for every meal. Thy parents were among those that did believe that something was owed to them. They did believe that they should have been able to give thy self and thy siblings a better life. Instead, your coffers were empty due to your parents greed and mismanagement."

Pushing him roughly from her lap, Ann stood and began pacing the room like a caged tigress. "But, this I still do not understand. My parents were good, God-fearing people. I do not understand how my father could break so with the church or how they could accuse innocent people. They used me to bring death!" Here, spectral tears, shining like so many diamonds began to slide down her pale cheeks. "So, what you are saying is it was all a lie. My parents told me to accuse innocent people. I did so because I was a good puritan girl. I even raised my brothers and sisters after they passed, leaving me nothing to feed the children on. I never married because I thought I was doing the right thing by continuing their work."

Ah, the dawn of realization. Sometimes, it is not a pretty sight. Realizing that all you thought you knew was no more than a sham. That people that you loved and were supposed to love you effectively killed your chances of ever having a life beyond the home before you were even of age to think of such things is a difficult blow to take.

"All I ever wanted was for them to love me. To be proud of me. When I began seeing witches amongst our friends, mother and father became so proud of me. They encouraged me to use my gift for the good of the town. I did what they asked because they were my parents. After they died, I needed help caring for the children. I needed someone to help me put food in their bellies. So, I went to the church and apologized. It was too late though. By then, everyone thought I was lying again, and no man would dare to marry me."

Mrs. Winkle twined herself about Ann's legs, but the girl was talking so swiftly and pacing so fiercly, she kicked her without even noticing.

"Now, poppet," She said, "Tis no good, fussin' over somethin' long since past. The question now is, now that you know what really 'appened, what do you intend to do about it?"

This stopped Ann in her tracks. The thought that she could do something about it clearly had never occurred to her. Now that it had, she finally looked peaceful. "I know what I must do.

Please, take me back. Let me make my amends as I should have, three hundred years ago."

Chapter Twenty-Three

We once again found ourselves at the final resting place of Sarah Goode. I blinked many times to clear the purple orbs from my vision.

When it did, I saw Ann, kneeling at the grave, her gaze fixed upon the marble face of the beautiful angel that adorned it.

"God, I understand now. How could I have been so blind? I cannot believe that I was foolish enough to behave so. If thou dost not see fit to allow me into thy divine present, I understand, and will happily walk the earth, committing myself to penance." With this, she bowed her head. For some strange reason, I felt the need to bow mine as well. As I did so, I could see my three companions do the same.

Suddenly, a beautiful silver flow lit up the night sky. I was terrified to look, yet I could not help myself. Lifting my head, I saw a woman, dressed in a flowing white gown, coming around the angel. I recognized her at once, although, I am not sure how. She was far more beautiful than the portrait in our home. This was Sarah Goode.

"Dear girl. The Lord dost work in mysterious ways." Her voice was rich and smooth as the finest chocolate. It made the hair along my spine stand on end, but the sensation was rather pleasant. "I have come to thee at last. And I only wish I could have come sooner."

Ann was dumbstruck, as were we all. I could not believe it. The victim coming to offer the killer some comfort.

She turned to me. "Bubbles, I thank thee. Thou didst thy grandfather and I very proud. Thou is true puritan stock. Never giving up. That was what made our people great. We came to this land, and carved a life for ourselves from this rough terrain. We lived on bread and water and sometimes, nothing at all. That is the lineage thou comes from and thou hast every right to hold thy head high with pride.

I blushed with this. If a feline could blush, that is. I don't think one could see it through all the fur. Turning to Nigel and Mrs. Winkle, she spoke again. "Faithful friends. I thank thee as well. Thou didst never give up, and after a rough start, learned to work together." Nigel was speechless, and I must say, I liked it. Mrs. Winkle merely gave a nod of her head. I don't think that at that moment, she was capable of anything else. Lasater stepped forward.

"Lasater. The faithful companion of my son. I thank thee most of all. Not only didst thou befriend an orphaned child, thou didst give thy life for his. It was thee that made the successful conclusion to this sordid tale possible, and you may come home now. Samuel misses you." The joy that lit him up was infectious. I was happy for my friend. Nay, my grandfather. He was finally going to be at peace in the arms of his friend, many years gone.

I looked now to Ann. The poor child was speechless with fright. More tears covered her lovely face as she waited for Sarah to address her.

As the elder woman turned to her, Ann did not give her a chance to speak first. Rushing forward on her knees, she clasped the hem of Sarah's dress and begin kissing it. "I beg thee, forgive me. I did not know, I did not know. I am sorry, so terribly sorry for the wrong I did thee and all the others. I..." But Sarah cut her off.

"I know child. I know. As does He." With this, she pointed skyward. "All He wanted was for you to realize that you had committed the wrong. Thou didst follow thy parents, but He gave thee free will to choose right from wrong. Now that thou hast seen the error of thy ways, thou may come home. A mother's love is a precious thing, and thou didst always have it. Though it did not come from the mother that bore thee." And she caressed the young girl's face.

Ann rose to her feet and hugged her. Turning to us, she bent down again. "Thank thee, all of thee. I cannot tell you what this means to me." Rising, she turned to Sarah again. Clasping hands, with Sarah holding Lasater, they disappeared.

Chapter Twenty-Four

To say that I was despondent following our adventures is a gross understatement. I had grown, as a spoiled, pampered house feline and was thrust into the most disagreeable role of family hero.

Our journey home was silent. None of us could speak. I was lost in thought that I had met my ancestor in the most unlikely of places and the mere fact was, I had grown to enjoy his company. Life would seem rather dull now that we had nowhere else to go. Our adventure was at an end.

The family did little to lighten my somber mood. Upon our return, there were no parades, not even a tender morsel in gratitude for the service we had done. I was pleased to see that we had a new member to the family. A healthy baby boy named Devin. He was beautiful and perfect in every way. Julia was radiant, lying in her bed among her many cushions. The sight put me in mind of Ann's mother, lying in her sick bed. And yet, the mood was entirely different. Julia was dreamy eyed, and completely in love with our new arrival.

Days stretched into weeks. Weeks stretched into months. I reveled in playing with the newest member of our clan, as did Mrs. Winkle. Nigel surprised even myself with his fierce loyalty to the child. He slept at the base of the bassinet to ensure that someone was always close by and he was never more than a room away from him at all times.

We three never discussed our adventure. Never spoke of the things that had transpired.

Occasionally, I would catch Mrs. Winkle or Nigel on the stair landing, staring up at the stained glass window. The design had changed. I had seen it myself one morning. I had taken to sleeping on the landing during the course of the events, and it was a habit I had yet to break. Truth be told, I did not want to.

One morning, as I rose just before the sun, I happened to look up. Any other morning, I would have seen the feet of a hanged woman near the base of that tree. Now, the scene was simply a tree. No more. No less. It was then that I knew the spirits were truly at rest.

You can imagine my surprise when I discovered that our adventures were not over. You see, during the course of the events of this work, Julia had finished writing her book. Apparently, it was very well received by the literary world.

She was hailed as the next great author, and I was glad for her. One morning, as we were all sitting in the breakfast nook, I overheard a most strange conversation. Apparently, Julia's book was a "big hit" overseas, and her publisher wished her to go there and sign books and whatnot. Well, she had always wanted to write a book based on the Emerald Isle, and she had arranged the tour during the summer so as to take the entire family with her. This included Nigel, Mrs. Winkle and myself. But that, dear reader, is another story.

The End.